A-Z

D0488375

Also by Barry Jonsberg

MY LIFE AS AN
ALPHABET

BARRY
JONSBERG

ALLEN&UNWIN

SYDNEY · MELBOURNE · AUCKLAND · LONDON

Australian Government

Australia **Council**
for the Arts

This project has been assisted by the Australian Government through the Australia Council for the Arts, its arts funding and advisory body.

First published in 2013

Allen & Unwin
83 Alexander Street
Crows Nest NSW 2065
Australia
  Phone: (61 2) 8425 0100
    Fax: (61 2) 9906 2218
  Email: info@allenandunwin.com
    Web: www.allenandunwin.com

A Cataloguing-in-Publication entry is available from
the National Library of Australia – www.trove.nla.gov.au

ISBN 978 1 74331 097 7

Teachers' notes available from www.allenandunwin.com
Cover image: Getty Images/WIN-Initiative
Set in 11.5 pt Stempel Garamond by Toolbox
This book was printed in August 2014 at McPherson's Printing Group,
76 Nelson St, Maryborough Victoria 3465.
www.mcphersonsprinting.com.au
20 19 18 17 16 15 14 13 12

For Janet and Steve

IS FOR ASSIGNMENT

A is for assignment.

I'm excited. Miss Bamford is my English teacher and she is the best English teacher in the world.

Wait. Wrong way – go back. I haven't personally experienced every teacher in the world [obviously]. I believe in precision, so I must refine my statement. It is more accurate to say that she's the best teacher *as far as I'm concerned*.

Miss Bamford is a small woman and she is between thirty and sixty years of age. I refuse to guess at ages. I asked her once, in the interests of accuracy, and she wouldn't tell me. She wears long and shapeless dresses so it's difficult to tell what her body is like. But she is probably thin. The one unmistakable thing about Miss Bamford is her lazy eye. It's her right one and it rolls around like it's skating on something slippery. This lack of control disturbs many students in my class. Sometimes she shouts at a student and, given her lazy eye, it's difficult to tell who she is yelling at. One eye dips and bobs like a maniac and the other glares at a non-specific location.

Douglas Benson – he's my friend in English – once said that she might have one lazy eye, but the other is hyperactive and should be on Ritalin. When I told Miss Bamford what he said, her eye flitted about even more than normal. You might assume Douglas and I got into trouble for that. But we didn't. I'll tell you about it later.

The assignment.

It's a recount. She wrote it on the board.

RECOUNT: Write about something that happened to you in the past.

Of course, anything that already happened MUST be in the past and I tried to point this out, but Miss Bamford ignored me and continued explaining the assignment. We have to write a paragraph about ourselves for every letter of the alphabet. Twenty-six paragraphs in total and each one starts with a letter of the alphabet, from A through to Z. She gave us an example.

A is for Albright. I was born in Albright,
which is a small town about forty kilo-
metres from Brisbane in Queensland,
Australia. Not much happens in Albright,
so my birth was a cause of much cele-
bration. People danced in the streets and
there was a firework display for two nights
running. Since then, the town has gone
back to sleep. Or maybe it is holding its
breath, waiting for me to do something
else, something equally spectacular…

I wrote Miss Bamford's example in my English book. Our school is in Albright, so I suppose she was making the example relevant. But I didn't like the way the example made false statements. I mean, no one's birth causes *that* amount of excitement. It doesn't happen, so I put my hand up to query the point. But one of the things that makes Miss Bamford such a good teacher is that she knows exactly what I'm going to ask before I ask it.

'Candice,' she said. 'In a recount, it is perfectly acceptable to play around with the truth a little. Sometimes the truth is too plain to entertain a reader, and your job in this assignment is to entertain. We've talked about this before, remember?'

I did remember and I would have understood her point if she had been talking about a narrative. But I thought a recount had to be factual. So she should have called it a narrative recount if that's what she wanted. I kept my hand up, but I think she didn't see it. It's difficult to tell with her eye. Anyway, Jen Marshall interrupted.

'Yeah, shut up, Essen,' she said, even though I hadn't actually said anything.

There are several girls [and boys] in my school who call me Essen. It's a phonetic representation of S.N., which is short for Special Needs. Many people think I have learning disabilities, but they are mistaken. I once wrote a note to Jen saying that everyone is special and everyone has needs, so her insult [because that's what she intended it to be] is wide of the mark. She simply glared at me, chewed her gum and ripped the note into little pieces. If I have to be honest – and I *do* have to be honest, it's something I cannot avoid – then I must confess that Jen Marshall is *not the sharpest tool in the shed*, as Rich Uncle Brian might say. But that's not her fault. And she is very, very pretty. So I like her. Then again, I like nearly everyone, as Mum often points out.

'Quiet!' barked Miss Bamford.

'Sorry, Miss. Are you talking to me?' said Jen, and

everybody laughed. Well, not everybody. Miss Bamford didn't. So, nearly everybody.

I went to the library at lunchtime to start my assignment. I often go to the library at recess and lunchtime because it's peaceful and the staff make me feel welcome. I have my own seat that the librarians reserve for me. They don't even mind if I occasionally eat a sandwich, despite the rules saying it's forbidden. I don't do it often, though, because rules are important. So I sat in my chair and thought about the assignment. A paragraph for each letter, and each paragraph portraying something about my life. Some of the letters would be difficult. Q, for example. And X. I have never had an X-ray, so that's not in the equation. But I decided I would worry about that later. A was obviously where I should start.

But the more I thought, the trickier the assignment appeared. I wanted to tell Miss Bamford about my life, but a paragraph for each letter just wouldn't do it. And that's when I got my best idea. I wouldn't do one paragraph. I would do multiple paragraphs for each letter. I've written eighteen paragraphs already [not counting this one] and I've barely even *started* on my life. If this was the entire assignment I would be up to R and no one would be any wiser about the life of Candice Phee. See? It's taken eighteen paragraphs [well, eighteen and a half] just to reveal my name. And I want to do a thorough job. Because this isn't just about me. It's also about the other people in my life – my mother, my father, my dead sister Sky, my penpal Denille, Rich Uncle Brian, Earth-Pig Fish and Douglas Benson From Another Dimension. These are people [with the exception of Earth-Pig Fish, who is a fish] who have shaped me, made me what I am. I cannot recount my life without recounting elements of theirs.

This is a big task, but I am confident I am up to it.

It will take time [I have plenty of that]. It will take perseverance [I have plenty of that, too].

Already I am worried I have not made a proper start, so I am going to copy out the first letter I wrote to my penpal, Denille. I make copies of all the letters I've sent to Denille, so I don't repeat myself and therefore bore her. Denille lives in America. In New York City. One of the teachers at my school received an email from a teacher-friend in New York asking for students interested in becoming penpals with students in her class. It is a project to learn about different cultures. I was matched with Denille. I have written to her twenty times in the last year. One letter every two weeks. This is the first. It tells Denille something about me and that is good because it will also tell *you* something about me. It is an informative start.

~

Dear Denille,

My name is Candice Phee and I am twelve years old. I attend school in Albright, Queensland, a small town forty-one-and-a-half kilometres from Brisbane. I suppose you don't know about kilometres, because Americans deal in miles. Forty-one-and-a-half kilometres is approximately twenty-six miles, I guess (I wrote 'I guess' because I understand this phrase is exceptionally popular in the United States. See, I'm trying to connect).

So. About me. Well, I'm kinda average height for my age ('kinda' is another attempt at linguistic connection) and I have long dirty-blonde hair. I don't mean 'dirty' in the sense that I don't wash it, because I do. Every day. But more in the sense of its natural colour, which, to be honest, makes it seem as if I don't wash it every day. Which I do. I have freckles. All over my face and my body. I can't go out in the sun unless I use cream with a sun protection factor of one zillion. Please understand that I am deliberately exaggerating for rhetorical effect. Dad says I should only go out in the sun when I'm wearing full body armour. He likes exaggeration as well. I have piercing blue eyes. Some people say they're my best feature. Actually, it's mum who says they're my best feature. She says they are like cornflowers (not to be confused with cornflour, which is white and used in baking).

I used to have a sister, but she died. This turned me into an only child.

I don't like many things that other twelve-year-olds like. Computers don't interest me. Most music is boring. I don't have a mobile phone because hardly anyone talks to me in real life, so why would anyone ring or text me? I only like movies that make me cry. I don't have friends who think they are friends. Apart from Douglas Benson From Another Dimension who I will tell you about in a later letter (see, I'm being mysterious).

What is it like being American? I only know from watching TV (another thing I'm not keen on) and it seems to me that being American must be very hard. Dad says Americans are arrogant, insular and can't name the countries to the south or the north of them. I'm not sure this is true (but if it is, the answer is Mexico and Canada). The TV

*shows I've watched give the impression of
Americans as shallow and obsessed with image.
Are you shallow and obsessed with image?*

*Albright is not like New York, even if
I don't know what New York is like. It's a
sleepy place. I've heard that New York never
sleeps, so we are a good match. With your
town never sleeping and mine constantly
sleeping, we will be like Yin and Yang.*

*Write soon. I very much look forward
to hearing from you.*

Your penpal,
Candice

~

I never got a reply to that letter. Actually, I never got a reply to any of the letters I've sent [twenty-one and counting] and I've wondered about that. Either Denille has changed her address and didn't give the postie her new one or she is too busy to write back. I suspect it's the latter. Americans are busy people. New York Americans must be even busier. But I like to think my letters might brighten up her day, so I continue to write regardless of her lack of reciprocation.

Rich Uncle Brian says it's probably better she doesn't reply. He thinks this way I cannot be disappointed. It upsets him when I am disappointed.

I wasn't there at my birth.

Well, I was, obviously, but I am an unreliable witness because I can't remember a thing about it. So, I must rely upon the reports of others who were present. It would have been wonderful if the actual witnesses to my birth–

  my mum

  my dad [not actually a *witness*, as such]

  Rich Uncle Brian

  the midwife

–had got together at some time to share their experiences. That never happened. For one thing, the midwife was a hospital employee and may not have been available for a family discussion. For another thing, Rich Uncle Brian and my dad are no longer on speaking terms, for reasons that may [or may not] become clear. But I have spoken to all of them about it at one time or another. Well, not the midwife, obviously. I don't even know her name, so I'll have to miss her out, unfortunately.

A couple of years ago, I asked Mum. She was having a good day.

'Mum? What was it like giving birth to me?'

Mum sipped her tea and put a hand over her eyes. There was no particular reason for this, since we were sitting in the front room and the curtains were closed. Mum often has the curtains closed. The light hurts her eyes.

'Your birth? It was like passing a basketball.'

This puzzled me for a moment. I thought she was referring to the game where one player passes the ball to another so she can score a hoop. I think that's what it's called. I thought she meant it involved teamwork. I kept quiet.

'What do you want to know, Pumpkin?'

Mum often calls me Pumpkin for reasons that have never been made clear. What reading I have done on the subject of nicknames [not much, I have to admit] doesn't throw a great deal of light on the enigma.

Apparently, in France it is common to call someone *'mon petit chou'* which means 'my little cabbage.' So it is acceptable, if you are of the Gallic persuasion, to refer to someone affectionately as a green, leafy vegetable. This is hard to understand. It is clear, however, that what with pumpkins and cabbages, people of different ethnic origins associate the world of gourd-like squashes/coleslaw ingredients with the warm and affectionate. It is strange. Then again, many things are strange but still ARE. What would Jen Marshall say if I called her an asparagus or a bok choy or a kohlrabi or a Jerusalem artichoke? She would slap me. Even if I meant it affectionately. *Especially* if I meant it affectionately. I once asked penpal Denille if it was the custom to show affection in the USA by referring to people as potatoes [for example], but like I said earlier, she hasn't replied, so I am still in the dark.

'Everything,' I replied.

'You were a tricky delivery.' Mum sighed. 'I was in labour for eighteen hours and when you finally arrived I was completely exhausted. I'd sworn that I wouldn't scream and carry on. I had done all my pre-natal classes and had practised the breathing, all the relaxation techniques.' She rubbed in a distracted fashion at her brow and closed her eyes. 'But when the time came, all my good intentions went out the window. I screamed.

I bellowed. I pleaded for an epidural. I had to fight Rich Uncle Brian for the gas and air, he was that disconcerted.'

'Where was Dad?'

'He was in Western Australia, attending a conference for the business. You arrived early. He thought he'd be back in time. He wasn't. Not for the actual birth. He made it to the hospital when you were about three hours old.'

'So Rich Uncle Brian stepped into the breach?'

'Yes. He held my hand while I screamed abuse at him and tried to tear the gas and air from his hand. You arrived in this world, Pumpkin, accompanied by pain, blood and tears. It was a violent entry.'

'Was I worth it?'

Mum opened her eyes.

'Every second, Pumpkin. Every second.'

~

Rich Uncle Brian's version was different. He picked me up from school and took me to a fast food restaurant for something lacking in taste and nutrition. This happens a couple of times a month. I nibbled on a beef burger of dubious origin while he looked out the window and jingled coins in his trouser pocket. Rich Uncle Brian does that a lot. It's a nervous habit.

'Rich Uncle Brian?' I said.

He turned his light blue eyes on me and stroked his moustache. He does that a lot as well.

'Yes, Pumpkin?' RUB is also keen on gourd allusions.

'Mum said I came into this world accompanied by pain, blood and tears. Is that how you remember it?'

He frowned.

'I do not, Pumpkin. I most emphatically do not.' He reached over the table and tickled me in the ribs. I think it was the same hand he used for coin-jingling. I pointed out to him that coins are the worst carriers of disease since they have so many owners in their lifetime and I did not relish being poked with a disease-carrying hand. He appeared slightly puzzled, but stopped. 'It was the most wonderful experience of my life,' he continued. 'You sailed into this world on a sea of love. You cruised through calm waters and berthed, with scarcely a ripple, into our hearts.' He made to reach over again, but thought better of it. 'And there, my sweet mariner, you remain. Docked in love.'

At one time Rich Uncle Brian was just Uncle Brian. But then he became rich and bought a yacht. Since then he occasionally uses nautical imagery, some would say to excess. I'm surprised he doesn't call me his sea cucumber. I finished my beef burger and digested his remarks. They were easier than the beef burger.

~

'Dad?' I said. 'Mum says I came into this world accompanied by pain, blood and tears, yet Rich Uncle Brian says I cruised through calm waters and berthed in everyone's hearts. Who is right?'

I'd had to tap Dad on the shoulder and get him to take off his headphones. He was sitting in his office in the shed. Dad spends a lot of time in the shed. He leaves for work at seven-thirty and doesn't come home until five at the earliest. Dad is self-employed. He has a white van with 'Home Bytes' custom-painted on the sides. Underneath there is a picture of an electronic gizmo and smaller letters: 'COMPUTER UPGRADES AND REPAIRS. I COME TO *YOU*.' He sometimes does work for local government, but mostly he visits people's homes and fixes their computers.

When Dad gets home he heats up his dinner in the microwave [Mum is usually in bed by this time] and then sometimes he takes his remote-controlled aeroplane out to our local park. He likes his remote-controlled plane. Dad says he enjoys the way he can control everything that it does. He says it is a welcome contrast to the rest of his life, but when I ask him to explain further he never says anything. Occasionally I go with him and watch the plane as it ducks and weaves around the branches of the trees. It is relaxing. Most of the time, though, I don't watch the plane. I watch Dad. His head arches back as he follows the flight pattern and his hands move quickly and with assurance over the control pad. He never talks and his eyes are always towards the sky.

Normally, Dad's muscles are tight and his eyes are sad, like those pictures of abused puppy dogs you sometimes see in advertisements for the RSPCA. They look resigned to the harshness of life, as if ill-treatment is an inescapable fact. But when he flies...when he flies, his muscles unknot and his eyes soften. He has the appearance of someone entirely at peace.

Most evenings, however, he heads out to his office in the shed. It is a cosy office, even though every surface is littered with machine bits. There is a bar fridge in a corner and he often has a beer while he types away on one of the computers. He has two huge screens on his desk. I don't know why he needs two. To be honest I don't really know what he does in there all the time. But sometimes I like to watch while he works. The computers don't have the same effect on him as the plane. His shoulders are hunched and one foot taps away on the concrete floor. So I don't really watch him.

One of his machines has a clear plastic case with lights that flash on and off, and I fix on that. The colours are red, blue, orange and green, and they make patterns that don't repeat. They are beautiful and much better than television.

Dad looked at me. His headphones hung around his neck like strange jewellery.

'Your Uncle Brian…' he said. If I was being particularly literary, then I suppose I should write 'he spat'. But I couldn't see any phlegm, so I think I will err on the side of precision. Dad took a deep breath and started again. 'Your uncle is not the most reliable person in the world.' Dad never refers to Rich Uncle Brian as his brother, or Brian or even Rich. It's always 'your uncle.' They have a history.

'Yes, but what's your view, Dad?' I asked.

His eyes flicked to the side and his foot tapped even harder.

'I wasn't there when you were born, Candice,' he said finally. 'I was too late.'

Then he put his headphones back on and returned to his typing. I thought I heard him mutter *the story of my life* under his breath, but I might have been mistaken. I am sometimes.

Dad is something of a mystery to me, but at least he doesn't call me any kind of vegetable, which is a welcome change.

So I still don't know much about the manner of my birth. Probably the only thing I learned was that people can view the same events in radically different ways. For Rich Uncle Brian, it was peaceful. For Mum it was traumatic. For Dad it was a reminder of something missed.

So B is for Birth. I was born. That's it.

IS FOR CHAOS

Classrooms are battlegrounds.

Students resist work. Generally. That is their job. Teachers encourage work. Generally. That is their job. I respect both sides. It makes the class a safe battleground when everyone knows their roles and tries to perform them. Of course, there are exceptions. Like the time Darren Mitford swallowed his pencil sharpener and nearly died. Our Maths teacher thought for a moment that Darren was being an idiot. Darren is an excellent idiot, so it was an understandable mistake. It takes a surprisingly short time for someone to turn from pink to purple to the colour normally associated with corpses. Darren didn't even have the breath to gurgle. He sat in his chair, mouth open, changing colour like a chameleon. When the teacher finally realised the seriousness of the situation, he jolted into action and performed a Heimlich manoeuvre. The sharpener shot from Darren's throat in an impressive blur of speed, ricocheted off a wall and pinged Susan Morris over the right eye. Stunned for a moment, she raised a hand to her brow, and when it came away red, she shrieked and fell to the floor. Darren meanwhile went from dark purple to light purple and finally pink again.

He still sucks pencil sharpeners. And almost everything else.

But generally at school there was a routine.

Douglas Benson broke it.

I sat in Miss Bamford's English class working on a comprehension exercise when the door opened and Miss Coolidge, the Assistant Principal in charge of curriculum, walked in. A boy shuffled at her side. She went through the ritual of introducing the boy [Douglas Benson] to the class and asked that everyone treat him with kindness and consideration. She said he was new to the area and didn't know anyone. He gazed at our sea of faces, wearing the haunted look of one who has just been publicly identified as being new to the area and not knowing anyone. He might as well have had a big bulls-eye painted on his forehead. Finally, he was allowed to sit down and Miss Coolidge disappeared to get on with the business of being in charge of curriculum.

Douglas Benson sat next to me.

He had to. It was the only unoccupied seat. No one ever willingly sat next to me. That was also part of the routine and I respected that. I picked up my pen and continued the comprehension task. A few minutes passed before I felt a tap on my arm. I looked up.

'Can you keep a secret?' whispered Douglas Benson.

'No,' I whispered.

'Oh.'

I went back to the comprehension. A minute later there was another tap.

'Not even a little bit?' whispered Douglas Benson.

'No,' I whispered.

'Oh.'

There was a third tap.

'Do you want to hear my secret anyway?' he whispered.

'No.'

'Oh.'

The bell went. It was lunchtime. Douglas Benson was in luck. He'd only been in class for ten minutes and he was getting a break. I packed my pens and pencils very carefully in my case. I was very careful because I hate it if my pens come into contact with my pencils. It's upsetting. There is a divider in my case [Dad made it for me] to make it easier for me to keep my pens and pencils separated. Douglas Benson watched me as I lined them all up so the pointy ends were facing the same way.

'Why do you do that?' he asked.

'Don't ask,' I replied.

'Okay,' he said.

'It's lunchtime,' I said.

'Is that your answer?' he said.

'To what?' I replied.

'To why you do that. Lining up your pens.'

This was getting too complicated, so I unpacked one of my pens and tore a sheet out of a notepad I keep just for these circumstances. This is what I wrote:

No. I told you not to ask me. It was
simply an observation that it's lunch-
time. How could 'it's lunchtime' be an
answer to why I line my pens up?

He read this with a screwed-up forehead. Well, he actually read it with his eyes, but his forehead *was* screwed up.

'Is it?'

'What?' I said.

'Lunchtime.'

'Yes,' I said. The conversation wasn't very exciting, but I so rarely have conversations at school that I was enjoying it. Maybe that was why I asked him what he was doing at lunchtime. I wouldn't normally dream of asking something like that, so I must have been stimulated by all our talk.

'What are you doing at lunchtime?' I said.

'I am working on a way of getting out of here,' he said.

I found this mysterious. 'That's mysterious,' I said.

'Is it?' he said.

'Yes. Because it doesn't take much working out,' I replied. This was a long sentence and I was too tired to add another, so I wrote another note: *You just go out the front door and there's a big gate*. I added a little drawing just to be helpful. I even put *YOU ARE HERE* on the here where we were.

'I didn't mean that,' he said.

'Oh,' I said. 'Sorry.'

'It's to do with my secret,' he said.

'Oh,' I replied. It is my experience that 'Oh' is a very useful word and much underrated.

I tore another sheet from my pad. I couldn't remember the last time I had used so many sheets in one day, let alone a couple of minutes. This is what I wrote:

If you like, you could come with me to the
library. The librarians keep a chair reserved
for me, but they wouldn't have one for you.
They let me eat sandwiches in there sometimes,
but I don't think you would be allowed. It is
against the rules. And I don't even know if you
have a sandwich. But you could come if you
want, despite the chair and sandwich thing.

I handed him the sheet.

'You're weird, aren't you?' he said.

'Yes,' I said. 'Certainly.'

'That's okay,' said Douglas. 'I'm weird, too. Maybe it's a good idea to stick together. We could be friends. Weird friends.'

I had plenty of friends already. Well…that depends on perspective. As far as I was concerned I had heaps of friends. As far as everyone else was concerned I didn't have a friend in the world. Does that make a difference? I'm not sure. Anyway, it would make a pleasant change to have a friend who also thought that I was a friend, so even though Douglas was always going to be a friend [according to my view of the world], he might actually be a *special* friend. That felt good.

'Yes,' I said. 'Good.'

I re-packed my pen and swung my backpack onto my back. It is called a backpack because that is where it belongs. Douglas trailed me through the corridors and up the library steps.

'Who is your best friend?' he asked.

I gave this some thought.

'You,' I said. I wasn't sure if this was strictly true. There was always penpal Denille, but she might be arrogant and deficient in terms of basic geography. The jury is still out.

~

I suppose it might not be obvious why I have called this chapter 'C Is For Chaos' [while Darren Mitford caused some, albeit temporarily, Douglas Benson From Another Dimension doesn't fit neatly into this category]. Hopefully, all will become clear...

My family. Mum, Dad and Rich Uncle Brian. It's clearly a complicated story, and I don't know all the fine details. In fact, I don't know many of the coarse details. Everyone has tried very hard to keep me in ignorance. I think that they think they are protecting me. But I would have to be living in a lead-lined coffin not to realise that everyone is miserable. I asked Mum and she said it was all water under the bridge. For a while I pondered scenarios involving buckets and cantilevers [I mean I know it's a saying, but sometimes I can't help myself]. Dad mutters darkly under his breath but refuses to be more specific. Rich Uncle Brian says we are weathering a storm.

Water flowing under bridges in a storm, while people mutter. Darkly.

It's not helpful.

Luckily, I have picked up information over the years, simply by pretending to be invisible. Adults always fall for this. They will talk freely if you just hang back and blend in with the wallpaper. If you have wallpaper. If not you have to blend in with the paint. What follows is part of the story. I believe there is more water that has yet to hit a bridge.

Dad and Rich Uncle Brian were once partners in a business, back when Rich Uncle Brian was just Uncle Brian. In fact, I think it started before I was born, so Uncle Brian wasn't even an uncle. Just Brian. It was a business involving computers. I know nothing about computers and don't care to learn. Which is strange since I hail from a genetic line of people who love the things. However, though I don't know much, I do know a little.

Dad – present-day Dad – builds computers and takes them apart. The original business didn't do that. Brian and Dad...Actually, Dad wasn't Dad then either. So Brian and James [who became my uncle and father respectively] devised software, the thing [I don't know exactly; don't ask me] that makes the machines run whatever the machines run. Word processing programs and such-like. They didn't pick up a screwdriver. They picked up pens and wrote code.

Any idiot who can manipulate Lego can put a computer together [I quote my Dad], but it takes talent to program [I quote Rich Uncle Brian]. Many people were doing it. The brothers' business was performing quite well, but it wasn't performing completely and utterly well. No one was buying yachts or fast cars with only two seats. Then Brian [aka Rich Uncle Brian] patented a piece of software that he designed. Here is where things get tricky and one person's truth apparently doesn't coincide with another person's truth. Dad doesn't believe Brian did all the designing. He thinks Brian used some of his ideas. Rich Uncle Brian, it seems, disagrees. Mum thinks that even if Rich Uncle Brian did invent the software, it was unfair to have patented it in just his name, since the brothers were in business together and should have shared.

It is easy to guess what happened. The software was a huge success [it has something to do with social networking – that's it, don't ask me any more] and money flowed in like stormwater under a bridge. But all the money flowed into Uncle Brian's pockets, making him Rich Uncle Brian. There was a court case. Nasty things, unforgivable things, were said. The business was sold to pay legal costs.

But, when it was all done and dusted, Uncle Brian was Rich Uncle Brian and Dad was broken and broke. Rich Uncle Brian bought a yacht. Dad bought a small white van and a remote-controlled aeroplane.

My family. Chaos. They're *almost* synonyms.

IS FOR DIMENSIONS

I want to tell you how I met Earth-Pig Fish.

About six months ago, Rich Uncle Brian took me to a fair. It wasn't one of those fairs with craft stalls, people in cowboy hats wrestling steers and wood-choppers turning logs into matchsticks. This was a fair in Brisbane and it had joyrides and dodgems and big dippers and fairy floss stalls. I like these sorts of fairs. I never go on the rides because I am afraid of heights, but that doesn't stop me enjoying myself. It's the lights and the smells and the bustle of people. There is some-thing magic about it. I've only been to two in my life.

So I was happy to watch Rich Uncle Brian go on

all the rides. I held his coat and waved at him as he slid past me on the Pirate Ship. Then he went on the Ghost Train. Twice. I wondered if that was what it was like to be a parent, smiling and waving as a shrieking person flashed past you with a wide grin and frightened eyes. I suspect there's a bit more to it than that.

When RUB had finished the rides we bought hot dogs and wandered along the rows of stalls. There were lucky dip stalls and a place where you had to throw a small ring around the neck of any one of dozens of bottles lined up. I had a go, but the ring kept bouncing off the bottles. It looked easy, but no one managed to do it, at least while I was there. Rich Uncle Brian was cynical.

'They design these things so you can't win, Pumpkin,' he said.

I thought he was probably right, but I also thought it wasn't worth mentioning. People were having fun. They were bathed in lights and clutching prizes or toffee apples or clouds of fairy floss on a stick. The fair was no place for cynicism.

We passed a shooting range. Metal ducks ran along three rows. They were battered and dented by experience, but kept on going. No one was shooting at them, so the man behind the counter was doing his best to get custom.

'C'mon, sir,' he yelled at Rich Uncle Brian. 'Try your

skill. Win a prize. Ten dollars a pop and every gun has sights.'

Rich Uncle Brian stopped.

'Yeah,' he said. 'Sights set to miss.'

The man was obviously offended. He put a hand over his heart.

'Not here, mate. Try for yourself. Five shots for free. If you miss, you walk away. If you hit, then give it a go. Whaddaya say?'

Rich Uncle Brian looked down at me. I shrugged and held out my hands for his jacket.

He hit ducks with four out of his five shots.

'Okay,' he said to the man behind the counter. 'Provided I use this gun.'

'Be my guest.'

Rich Uncle Brian spent eighty dollars trying to win a prize. Well, he won a prize every time, but the prize was a pencil with a fluffy thing stuck to its end. It was probably worth twenty cents. He had his eye on the major prize – a huge stuffed animal that might have been a gnu or a camel with severe disabilities. And Rich Uncle Brian wasn't giving up until he had it. I might have pointed out that it was probably worth about forty dollars, but I suspected that wasn't the point. This was about proving himself. Mum says that men are just little boys deep down. Sometimes not so deep down.

Sometimes not deep at all, but right on the surface. He could've bought a whole Toys R Us shop, being Rich Uncle Brian, but this wasn't about money. I held his jacket and watched the ducks fall.

'Hah!' said Rich Uncle Brian in triumph, one hundred dollars later. The man handed over the deformed camel/gnu and RUB passed it on to me. I knew he would.

'I don't want it, Rich Uncle Brian,' I said. 'It's vile.'

His face crumpled in disappointment. I felt bad, but I couldn't lie to him. The toy *was* horrible.

'But I won it for you, Pumpkin,' he said. 'If you don't like this, what do you like?'

'That,' I said, and pointed.

A goldfish in a plastic bowl. It sat on a shelf to the right of the ducks, which were still going round cheerfully despite being targets. I say it sat, but that was the bowl. The fish was swimming. It was gold and beautiful.

'We'll have that instead,' said Rich Uncle Brian, pointing.

The man shook his head.

'No can do, mate,' he replied. 'That's not a prize. That's my pet. Time was, you could give away goldfish as prizes, but no more. Against the law. I could lose my licence.'

'Your pet?' asked Rich Uncle Brian. There was that cynicism in his voice again.

'Yup. Very attached to him. Very.' The man stroked

his chin thoughtfully. 'Then again, if the price was right...not against the law to sell your pet, is it?'

Rich Uncle Brian sighed.

'How much?'

'A hundred bucks.'

'WHAT?'

'Very attached to him, I am.'

Rich Uncle Brian looked down at me and then at the fish and then at the man. He sagged a little and got out his wallet. Again.

'Tell you what,' he said to the man. 'Fifty and you can have your stuffed prize back.'

'Deal.'

Rich Uncle Brian handed over the cash and the gnu/ deformed camel and the man handed over the fish and the bowl.

'Tell you what, mate,' said the man. 'Since you've just bought the world's most expensive fish – about ten thousand dollars a kilo I reckon – then I'll throw in the bowl for free.'

Rich Uncle Brian smiled, but it didn't come out right. It was like one of those smiles when someone has pointed a camera at you for half an hour and neglected to press the shutter.

Later, in the car as we drove home, he asked me what I was going to name it.

'Earth-Pig,' I said. Rich Uncle Brian sighed.

'It's the translation of the Afrikaans word "aardvark",' I continued. 'It is an anteater and means earth pig.'

'Is there any reason, Pumpkin, why you want to name a goldfish after an African anteater? I mean, I can't think of too many similarities. Colour, size, presence or absence of gills, that sort of thing.'

'You're right, Rich Uncle Brian,' I said. 'But it's the first proper word in the dictionary.'

The dictionary is my favourite book. I often read it at bedtime. It has thousands of different words and it doesn't try to tell a story, and fail. It just deals in words for their own sake. It is pure. The only other thing I read is books by Charles Dickens. He has taken many of the trickiest words from the dictionary and put them in an interesting order. This is clever and admirable.

'Won't it be confused by being called a pig?'

'Maybe,' I said. 'It could suffer an identity crisis.' I thought for a few minutes. 'I will call it Earth-Pig Fish. That is a good name.'

We drove in silence for about twenty minutes.

'Do you know what the best thing about you is, Pumpkin?' said Rich Uncle Brian finally.

'No.'

'You sing your own song, Pumpkin, and you dance your own dance. You see the world differently from the rest of us. And you know? Sometimes I think I wish everyone saw it the same way you do. I know the world would be a better place.'

I didn't say anything. But I must admit I was very surprised. He didn't use one maritime metaphor.

~

Douglas Benson told me his secret ten minutes into lunch. The librarians lent him a chair, though they didn't encourage him to eat. They didn't forbid it either, mind.

'I am from another dimension,' he said.

'That's nice,' I replied.

'Well, not really,' he said. 'You see I like the dimension I came from whereas this one sucks big-time.'

I considered that for a while, but it didn't do any good. I still had no idea what he was talking about.

'I have no idea what you are talking about,' I said.

Douglas Benson has an interesting face. His eyes crowd towards the middle as if they are trying to merge together but are prevented from doing so by the barrier of his nose, which is larger than you'd wish if you were designing it from scratch. He has eyebrows like hairy caterpillars, and a mouth that is very wide. His fingers are thin and long, though they are not part of his face, obviously. He would make a good pianist. Anyway, Douglas's interesting face was screwed up in concentration.

'You know about M-theory, I imagine,' he said.

That wasn't a question so I said nothing.

'It's a multi-dimensional extension of string theory in which all universes – the multiverse, if you like – are created by collisions between p-branes…'

'Pea brains?'

'Yes.' He spelled it. He said some other things, but I missed some of the detail because I was thinking about colliding pea brains creating universes. We have a lot of pea brains at my school. Remember pencil-sharpener-sucker Darren Mitford? He and other pea brains often collide in the playground, particularly when they play ball games. I enjoyed the image of their collisions spawning universes inhabited by pea-brained sports enthusiasts. I shook my head and tried to focus on what Douglas was saying. '…operating with either eleven or twenty-six dimensions. As a result of these collisions a universe is created within its own D-brane, and there are, clearly, an infinite number of such D-branes, and therefore an infinite number of universes, of which this is just one. Now the point is…'

I was glad he was getting to the point because my brain was hurting. Or was it my brane?

'…each universe is locked from the other universes because each object, including forces and quantum physics itself, is restricted to its own D-brane. Except gravity. You see? Except gravity. The only force not restricted to its own D-brane. Thus it is through gravity that transference between universes is possible. It is how I came to be here. Consequently, gravity is the key to me returning.'

He gazed at me triumphantly. I gazed back at him blankly. He sighed.

'You haven't understood a word I've said, have you?'

I ripped a sheet of paper from my pad and extracted a black pen from my pencil case. If ever there was a time for such a manoeuvre, it was now.

On the contrary (I wrote). I understood
nearly all the words you said. 'Brane' was,
I think, the only exception, unless it is a
contraction of 'membrane', in which case
I understood ALL the words you said. Words
are not a problem. It is their order which can
be. For example, here are some simple words:
jumped; desks; happy; will; aardvarks; in;
back. All can easily be understood in isolation
(maybe not aardvark – it is an anteater
indigenous to South Africa). But if I put
them together thus – back desks in aardvarks
happy will jumped – then you would have
difficulty understanding my meaning and
might interpret it as a particularly bizarre

pronouncement from Yoda, of Star Wars
fame. So it is with your expressions, Douglas.
I understood the words. I missed the meaning
entirely. Explain in simple terms, please.

Douglas read this and frowned again. I think he might be a huge fan of frowning.

'Okay,' he said. 'This universe you know. All the stars, all the space. Everything that exists. It is not the only one. There are an infinite number of such universes. Millions upon millions, billions upon billions. And then more…'

'I know what infinity means.'

'Okay. That means there are an infinite number of Earths. And each will be slightly different. There will be an infinite number of Candices, for example. In one you might have brown hair. In another…well, the combinations are…infinite.'

So somewhere, I thought, *there is a world where penpal Denille replies to my letters. Just my luck to be in one where she doesn't.*

'The other universes are separated from this one,' he continued, 'not by space and time, but by a different dimension. I came through that dimension. Another universe.'

'How?' I asked. It seemed a reasonable question. And it was short.

'You wouldn't understand. It involves manipulating dimensions and invoking gravity, of course.'

'How?' I asked. I was on a roll.

'I jumped out of a tree.'

I could understand that bit.

'And found yourself here?' I asked.

'Yes.'

'So jump out of another tree and go back.'

He sighed and frowned, confirming my earlier suspicions.

'It's not as easy as that,' he said.

Nothing is, I thought.

IS FOR EARTH-PIG FISH

Dear Denille,

I have a goldfish called Earth-Pig Fish.
She lives in a bowl on my bedside cabinet.
I say 'She', but to be honest, I can't be
certain about her gender. I think you need
to have studied veterinary science for a
number of years, since there are no outward
indications, at least not that I can spot.

Earth-Pig Fish is an interesting fish. She
doesn't do anything that most people would
categorise as interesting. In fact, she is fairly
predictable and swims around her bowl, opening

*and closing her mouth. Sometimes she goes
clockwise and sometimes she goes anti-clockwise.
I do not think there is a pattern and I should
know because I have spent a lot of time with
her. What I think is interesting is how she
MIGHT view her world. I stressed the word
'might' because obviously I can't know for sure.*

Bear with me on this.

*Look at the world from Earth-Pig Fish's
perspective. As far as she knows, her universe is
bounded by plastic. She cannot experience life
outside it (because she would die). She probably
thinks it's an okay universe, if only because she
doesn't know any other. BUT (and this is my
point) occasionally a human face (MY face)
looms up outside her universe and interacts with
her. I mouth things through the plastic. I talk
to Earth-Pig Fish a lot, for reasons I don't want
to go into right now. What does she make of
this? Does she think, maybe, that I am God
trying to communicate with her? I balloon
into view (on account of the refractive nature
of certain types of plastic) and then I balloon
out again. This could be a mystical experience
for her. Does she think I am giving her a
message about how she should live her life?*

Maybe. Maybe not.

*But what if the God so many people
believe in is something like that? A presence
ballooning into our consciousness from
time to time – a presence we think is telling
us something profound, but is actually
only thinking it's time to clean us out?*

*I have a friend. Douglas Benson From
Another Dimension. I sometimes think he feels
like he is swimming around in a bowl and wants
to know what it is like on the other side of the
plastic. Sometimes I think we all feel like that.*

I would be interested in your views.
Your penpal,
Candice

~

About three weeks after I first met Douglas Benson
From Another Dimension, he invited me round to his
house. For afternoon tea. This was both amazingly
exciting and deeply troubling. Exciting, because no
one had ever invited me to afternoon tea before, and
troubling because, as Rich Uncle Brian has often remarked, I can be somewhat socially challenged.

I say it was my first invitation, but that is not strictly
true. I was once invited to a birthday party when I was

six, but I remember nothing about it. According to Mum I refused to speak and spent the whole time sitting under a tree, mumbling to worms. I was NOT the life and soul of the party, though it's possible the worms enjoyed my company. I cannot say with any certainty. What is clear, however, is that after that everybody human gave me up as a hopeless case.

So I was excited by Douglas's invitation and scared I would ignore his parents and talk to invertebrates [unlikely, I admit, since invertebrates are rarely invited to afternoon teas].

'Is it okay with your mum and dad?' I asked.

'They are NOT my mum and dad,' snarled Douglas. His mouth twisted in a fashion reminiscent of a snarly creature – a vicious dog, for example – so I feel justified in describing him so. 'They are facsimiles of my real mother and father who are in another dimension.'

'Ah, yes,' I said. It's difficult to know what to say in these circumstances, so I hummed for a few seconds. 'Do they *know* they are facsimiles?' I added after I ran out of hums.

'They think I am mad,' said Douglas. 'I tried to explain the situation to them logically. That I had arrived from another dimension and that, due to some law of the multiverse that conserves matter, their son is now in my universe, living with *my* parents. I told them my *real* mother was a quantum physicist and my *real* father a famous experimental musician. They refused to believe me.'

'Fancy that,' I said.

'They took me to the hospital. Some idiot in a white coat, hearing that I had fallen from a tree, pronounced that I was suffering from loss of memory caused by a blow to the head. It is unscientific and, frankly, insufferable.'

I hummed a bit more.

'What do your facsimile parents do?' I asked. This seemed safe ground.

'The female is a postie and the male is a nurse,' snarled Douglas.

I was impressed with his snarling. It was really very good.

I have never known a quantum physicist. I'm not sure what they do, but it doesn't seem to have much impact on the world. A postie, however, is different. Useful. She delivers letters and parcels. This is definitely a good thing. Without posties, penpal Denille couldn't read my letters. Without posties we would constantly check our letter boxes and be constantly disappointed. The world would be a sadder place. I was tempted to point this out to Douglas Benson From Another Dimension, but felt it wasn't the right time. I believed that we would certainly disagree on the respective merits of posties as compared to quantum physicists.

I am not qualified to talk about experimental musicians, so I kept quiet on that subject as well.

'So is it okay with your facsimile parents?' I asked.

'Is what okay?'

'Me coming to afternoon tea.'

'Oh, they *love* the idea,' said Douglas in a bitter tone of voice. He was an unhappy boy. Bitter tones of voice and excessive snarling are, to my mind, clear evidence of this. 'They think it's a sign my mental health is improving. You know, having friends.'

I felt their optimism might be dashed once they met me, but again I kept my own counsel.

'I will talk to my mother,' I said. 'She's not a facsimile. At least, not as far as I am aware.'

~

I talked to my mother.

First, I had to tap gently on her bedroom door. When I come home from school, the house is generally quiet and Mum's bedroom door is generally closed. Sometimes I don't see her until the morning when she makes me breakfast. Sometimes I think she might be an endangered species. Conservationists could get very excited and talk in hushed tones when they spot her.

I rarely intrude when she is in her room, but this was an emergency and she had told me I could knock if there was an emergency. There was no immediate response. I was thinking about knocking again when I heard a faint, 'Come in.' I opened the door gingerly, since even the squeak of a rusty hinge can cause Mum pain. The bedroom was dark and smelled of something that had spent a long time out of the sunshine. I waited a few moments to allow my eyes to adjust. Mum was sitting up in bed, a lumpy shadow among other lumpy shadows. I tiptoed over.

'Mum?' I whispered.

'Yes, Pumpkin?' she replied in a voice soaked in weariness.

'I have been invited round to afternoon tea tomorrow by a friend from school. Can I go, please?'

The lumpy shadow sat up straighter. A shadow that was probably a hand rubbed at a shadow that was probably her eyes.

'A friend, Pumpkin? That's brilliant. Who is she?'

Her voice was tired, but tinged with excitement. Mum has spent considerable time hoping I would find a friend who would invite me to afternoon tea. As the years passed I think she gave up all hope. I believe this has contributed to the weight of sadness she carries, and naturally I have felt guilty.

'The she is a he, Mum,' I replied. 'Douglas Benson From Another Dimension. He is incredibly strange as well.'

'You are NOT strange, Pumpkin.'

I didn't say anything. We have had these conversations many times. Mum insists I am not strange. I know I am. There is little point in arguing about this. Especially if it makes Mum unhappy, which it does for reasons I haven't yet worked out.

'Okay,' I said. 'Can I go?'

'I will need to ring his mother,' she said.

I had the phone in my hand already. I also had the number that Douglas had given me on a sheet of paper. I pride myself on being well organised. I held out both the phone and the sheet of paper.

'Make me a cup of tea, Pumpkin,' she said as she took them. 'I'll ring and then come out to the kitchen.'

'You should be aware that she is his facsimile mother,' I said. 'I leave it to you to decide on the correct form of address under these circumstances.'

I left to make the tea, which is something I enjoy doing.

IS FOR FRANCES [SKY]

Rich Uncle Brian says newborn babies look like bull-dogs. Most of the time, I know what he means. The hanging jowls and lolling heads.

But Sky was different. Her cheeks were rounded and covered with soft down. When I ran my hand along her cheek it was like stroking a peach, faintly warm and the texture of satin. She smelled of powder and milk and her. I would bury my nose in her neck and fill my nostrils. I inhaled her while she made snuffling noises.

Sky was my sister and I first saw her when I was five. When I think back to that time, I picture it in snapshots. Separate images connected by blanks, like white, empty spaces in a photograph album. Only occasionally do they spool together to form a story. I remember looking up at Mum in the kitchen. She was doing something with flour and her hands were dusty so she couldn't touch me. But she was smiling and one white hand rested on the swell of her stomach. I remember Mum and Dad talking about the new baby and the changes ahead. They tried to make me feel comfortable about what was going to happen but they needn't have bothered. I was excited, not because I knew what to expect [I was five. You don't know what to expect at five. You don't know what to expect at twelve. Maybe you never know what to expect], but because our household was alive with happiness. It bubbled and made us glow. The sun was brighter then, the grass greener, the clouds whiter.

So maybe Sky *did* look like a bulldog and it's only my memory that has re-formed her. I don't think so, however. I have photographs, and though they sometimes lie, I do not believe so in this case. Not in this case.

I remember nothing of Mum going into labour. I cannot remember Dad driving to the hospital. My first sight of Sky, though, is vivid still. A tiny arm poked from a tiny blanket. It was fleshy and rounded and ended in a clump of perfect fingers. It was hard to

believe that a fingernail could be so small yet so beautifully finished. Mum sat up in a bed so white it glowed.
It was as if she was partly buried in a snow drift. Her
hair was wet and stuck to her head. One dark tendril
curled against a pale cheek. She held something small
and pink against her chest. The baby, too, had a lick of
dark, wet hair that clung to her skin. I remember thinking that this small thing was a part of my Mum, chipped
off in some way. The hair was the connection.

'Say hello to your sister, Pumpkin,' said Mum. Her
voice was smiling, but I couldn't take my eyes from the
baby. I didn't say hello. I simply stared.

Dad leaned in. He put his index finger against the
baby's fist. Her fingers curled and then clamped down.
She clutched his finger as if her life was anchored to it.
It was then that my heart first lurched and something
powerful was born within me. Such a tiny thing. Such
a tiny, perfect thing.

'Do you want to hold her, Candice?' said Dad.

I shook my head.

'It's okay,' he added. 'We'll help you. You won't
drop her.'

I stared.

Dad leaned in again.

'Frances,' he said. 'Meet your big sister Candice.'

Mum shifted her grip and turned the baby's face

towards me. Her eyelids were partly closed, her lips an exaggerated bow, impossible eyelashes against impossible skin. And then she opened her eyes and looked straight into mine. I was told afterwards that newborn babies cannot focus properly, that it is something they learn later. I do not believe it. She looked into my eyes and saw something there. Hers were a pale blue, though other colours shifted within them. I felt I was staring into someone who had no end, that the mind behind the gaze went on forever. I was staring into the sky and I knew that was her name. Frances was a label, but Sky was who she was. Who she will always be.

Rich Uncle Brian lived in a large house with eight bedrooms that no one else ever stayed in. He was alone. Mum, Dad, Sky and I lived in a small house with only two bedrooms. It is where we live still. Mum and Dad put a cot in their bedroom and Sky slept there for her first six months. She woke at least three times a night because she was hungry. Sometimes she woke when she wasn't hungry and Dad walked her round and round the house, her head peeping over his shoulder. He jogged a little as he walked so her head bounced slightly. He murmured to her. I followed him. Whenever Sky woke, I woke. Occasionally, I would wake slightly before she did, or maybe it would be more accurate to say slightly before she cried. Perhaps we always woke at the same time. But I knew when I glanced at my bedside clock and saw it was 12.30 or 2.55 or 4.13 that she was awake. I'd climb out of bed and go into Mum and Dad's room, just as Sky was starting to sniffle and cry. At first, Mum and Dad took me back to bed, but it was never any use. Even when they forced me to stay in my room, I couldn't sleep until she'd drifted off. After a while they stopped trying to keep me out of the room. I watched when Mum breastfed her. I followed behind Dad when he took Sky on her jiggly tour of the house. I helped with the changing duties. I became good at cleaning her tiny bottom and fitting it with a fresh nappy.

Sky smiled whenever she saw me. She smiled even when she was too young to smile, when I was told it was merely wind contorting the face. She smiled.

'Pumpkin, aren't you tired?' said Mum one morning over Weet-Bix.

'No, Mummy,' I said.

'It's just that all of us are having broken sleep, sweetie. Why don't you leave Frances to us and get a decent night's sleep?'

'I just wake up,' I said. 'Whenever she wakes, I do. And I can't go back to sleep then, Mummy. I just can't. So do you know what I think we should do?' I talked a lot more then. I didn't even wait for Mum to reply. 'I think we should put Sky's cot in my room. She should sleep with me. That way Daddy might get more sleep. He told me he's nearly fallen asleep when he's been driving and that is bad. I'll wake you up when Sky wakes up, so it'll be the same as now, except I'll get to sleep in the same room as her. Please, Mummy? Please?'

Mum and Dad exchanged a look, but didn't say anything. And another two months went by before they moved Sky's cot into my room.

She died four weeks later.

It would be good in a way – a literary way, I suppose – to say all the details of that evening have been fixed permanently into my memory. Or, given that I had a special bond with Sky, to say I had some warning about what would happen when I fell asleep on the fourteenth of June, two days before my sixth birthday. But it wasn't like that. It wasn't like that at all.

Mum read me a book as always. She kissed me on the forehead and told me to sleep well and to make sure the bed bugs didn't bite. Dad tickled me on my side. Then they both went to Sky's cot and bent over her sleeping form. My nightlight cast a pale red glow over the scene. I think I remember that Mum's and Dad's hands felt towards each other and their fingers entwined as they watched their youngest daughter. But maybe that is just memory playing tricks. Memory does that. And I was tired. My eyes were heavy and closing even then.

The room was hazy somehow, as if I were seeing under water. Then, nothing. I woke so violently that I sat up in bed in one movement. My heart was thudding, the pulse of blood loud in my ears. The nightlight still cast its rosy glow, but the moon also washed my bedroom in silver. I glanced at my bedside clock, but the numerals were flashing on 2.22. A power cut maybe. I had no idea of the time. I put my feet on the floor, snuggled my toes into ridiculous slippers that were in the shape of bunnies' heads and padded over to Sky's cot.

She lay on her back and her eyes were open. Moon-shadows and nightlights play tricks, as memories do, and for a moment I thought I saw her gaze shift and settle on my face. But the moment passed and I saw... nothing. The blue of her eyes was as intense as ever, but now there was no depth within them. It was as if the sky had become a shield, a plate of colour that was in one dimension only. I touched her face. It was warm, but my fingers sensed the heat departing.

Then all I could hear was screaming. I suppose it was mine.

No one talks about that night. I suppose there isn't a great deal to say. Many months later, Mum and Dad took me to a man who tried to get me to say something about it, but I had lost interest in talking by then. After a while, we carried on as a family. Not like everything was the same. It wasn't and we knew that. But we carried on because…well, what choice do we have?

I'm twelve years old and smart, apparently. I know what people think. That I blame myself for what happened to Sky and that my strange behaviour stems from guilt. I'd put pressure on Mum and Dad to let Sky sleep in my bedroom. Would she have died if she'd stayed in Mum and Dad's room? Was it all, in some peculiar fashion, a way of punishing myself for imaginary crimes? It would explain a lot. My writing of notes, rather than talking to people I don't know well. Some of my…obsessions.

But I don't blame myself. It wasn't my fault. Sky died of cot death. Sudden infant death syndrome is the medical term, though that explains nothing because no one knows why it happens. It just does. For no reason. No one's to blame.

Unfortunately the human mind doesn't work that way. Logic is no good here. Candice feels she is to blame and that is the important thing. But all I can do is repeat: *I know it wasn't my fault.*

But *it* is unbearably sad.

Families are fragile. Mine did not die when Sky did, but it took a battering and came out bruised and limping. It was the start of when things fell apart.

Mum's breast cancer. Dad's increasing distance

from everything except the computers in his shed and a faintly buzzing silhouette in the sky.

I never saw them touch hands after that night. Now I am surrounded by unhappiness. Mum. Dad. Even Rich Uncle Brian.

That is not my fault either.

But maybe I can do something about it.

Before the last traces of warmth flee my family too.

. . . .

IS FOR GRAVITY

. . . .

'This is it,' said Douglas Benson From Another Dimension. 'My passport home.'

'Wow!' I said, and meant it.

It looked like a tree, but apparently it was a passport home. It was a big, spreading passport with a gnarly trunk and loads of branches. Leaves blocked the sky and there was a bare patch of earth at the base where the grass did not grow. I stood on that patch and craned my neck. I made small cooing noises and hoped they sounded like appreciation. I had never seen a portal to another dimension before and the protocols were beyond me.

'How does it work?' I asked after a suitably awe-struck pause.

Douglas looked at me as if I were crazy, which was a little strange since I wasn't the one claiming that a spreading tree was a gateway to another dimension. *But then*, I thought, *I am crazy* – so I suppose he was entitled.

'I climb into its branches and jump,' he said.

'Hi tech,' I replied.

We were in his garden. I had come round for our afternoon tea date. Dad dropped me off, and when I had approached the house I had seen Douglas sitting under his passport, though at that time I'd thought, in my innocence, that it was a tree. Inside his house, I imagined, were facsimile parents, and I was nervous about meeting them so it was good to chat awhile and delay. I'd hoped to spy a postie's bike in the yard, but there was no evidence of one, which was disappointing. Still, I reasoned to myself, you can't have everything. A portal *and* a postie's bike was probably asking for too much.

'Come for a walk with me,' said Douglas. 'I want to show you something and the facsimile parents have informed me food will not be ready for another forty-five minutes.' His lip curled slightly when he made the parent reference. His eyes might also have flashed, but

I'm not prepared to swear to that in a court of law, so it's safer to stick with the lip-curling.

'Okay,' I said.

Douglas lived five-and-a-half kilometres outside Albright in a five-hectare block. Dad had driven up a rutted path, avoiding assorted chooks and one small lake. We retraced that journey up the path. It was a beautiful afternoon. The sky was clear and birds sang. It wasn't difficult to imagine we were the only people in the world. Douglas said nothing for ten minutes, and although I like silence, generally speaking, I had questions that were, if not exactly burning, definitely smouldering around the edges.

'Douglas,' I said. 'If travelling through dimensions happens when you jump out of a tree, are possums doing it all the time?'

He sniffed.

'It's not *just* jumping out of a tree, Candice,' he replied. 'There are other things involved and the maths is quite tricky.'

'Oh,' I said. I was a bit tired from my question. We walked for another minute or two.

'Do you have a pad and a pen with you?' he asked.

'Yes.' I knew that interaction with facsimile parents was inevitable and had come prepared.

'I'll draw you a diagram when we get there,' he said.

'Okay.'

There wasn't far away as it turned out. We'd veered off the driveway and wandered down a rough path through thick bushland, the kind of path that animals make when they can be motivated. The bushland wasn't very interesting – flat and crowded with spindly gums – so I was surprised when we came to a clearing. Surprised and alarmed, since we were virtually on the edge of a ravine. I say 'ravine', but that might be flattering it somewhat. Then again, I am afraid of heights, so even modest drops are ravines to me. I took a couple of tentative steps forward and cautiously peered over the edge. Slabs of rock lined the sides and forty metres below a small stream trickled in a picturesque fashion. I quickly stepped back. It's not that I don't like small picturesque trickling streams, but I prefer them when they are on my level. Ideally in a photograph. Douglas sat close to the edge and I joined him. Perhaps a metre behind.

'Pretty,' I said to his back, though I wasn't referring to that. And the scenery was pretty. It was a little surprise, like finding a bright stone in a pile of manure. That, I should stress, has never happened to me [possibly because I have never looked].

'It's nice here,' said Douglas. 'I often come here just to think.'

I was pleased to learn that Douglas had brought me to his special private place. It felt like an honour. I shuffled forward on my bottom so that I was nearly level with him.

'May I use your pad and pen?' he asked.

I produced them from my bag. He found a clean sheet and drew a line.

'What's that?' he said.

'A line,' I replied. It wasn't difficult.

'Correct. A line. One dimension.' He drew another three lines and lifted the pad towards my face.

'And that?'

'A square,' I replied. 'Or maybe a rectangle.'

'Correct. Two dimensions.' He scribbled some more.

'A cube,' I said, without being asked. I was on a roll.

'The illusion of a third dimension.' Then he went a bit mad with the pen. Lines appeared all over the place.

'And this?' he asked when he'd finished.

I screwed up my eyes and probably my forehead. I might even have tilted my head to one side.

'A mess?' I suggested.

'A tesseract,' he said. At least I got three of the letters right and in the correct order. 'If a cube is a square taken into the third dimension, then a tesseract is a cube taken to the fourth dimension. For obvious reasons it's difficult to draw.'

'I thought time was the fourth dimension,' I said.

'No,' he replied.

'Oh,' I said.

'What I'm trying to explain is that to travel between alternative worlds I need to take the tesseract to a fifth, sixth, seventh, eighth and then a ninth dimension, wrap myself within that construct and then use gravity to effect the journey.'

'That's where the tree comes in,' I suggested.

'Correct.' He sighed and placed the pad down on the ground. 'That's how I got here. Logically, it's how I should get back.'

'But?'

Douglas gazed out over the ravine for a few moments. He cupped his chin in a hand.

'Timing is everything,' he said. 'It must be at six-thirty in the evening. I've been over the maths time and time again. But it doesn't work.'

'Any idea why not?'

'The only solution I can come up with is that gravity has a slightly different quality in this world.'

'So?'

He thought for a moment or two.

'So maybe I need to jump from somewhere higher than a tree,' he whispered. It was as though he was talking to himself. Douglas peered over the edge of the ravine once more and suddenly the afternoon felt chilly. I hugged myself.

~

Douglas's mum was called Penelope and she was very pleasant. Facsimile Penelope. When she found out I was interested in her work, she said she would take me for a ride on her postie bike, but it never happened. She was small with a face like a walnut. Probably a result of riding around all day in the sun. Douglas's facsimile dad was called Joe and he had big ears and a bigger smile. I liked them. The parents I mean, not the ears, though I quite liked them too. We even had a good conversation before I had to get my pad and pen out.

'Do you like vegetables, Candice?' asked Penelope.

'Yes. Thank you.'

'Roast beef?'

'Yes. Thank you.'

'Gravy?'

'Yes. Thank you.' I was feeling confident.

'Is it okay if they are all on the same plate?'

I was ready for the yes, thank you, but the question stopped me in my tracks. I must have looked puzzled because Penelope continued.

'It's just that your mum told me that you like to have things a certain way, and Douglas mentioned your pencil case.' My puzzlement clearly hadn't diminished because she went on. 'The way you like to have everything lined up just so.'

I didn't say anything.

'So I wondered whether you were okay about having different colours of food on the same plate.'

I might have raised an eyebrow. Possibly two.

'You *are* autistic, aren't you?'

'No,' I said.

It was facsimile Penelope's turn to look puzzled.

'Then what are you?' she asked.

'I'm me,' I said.

~

Dad had arranged to pick me up at seven, so I had time to watch Douglas make his attempt at returning home. Penelope and Joe didn't join us outside. I had the impression this was a spectacle they had witnessed before and were less than impressed.

Douglas climbed the tree with a practised air and balanced on one of the lower boughs. He glanced at his watch and closed his eyes. It was obvious he was concentrating fiercely, doing things with tesseracts taken to higher dimensions. I stood well clear. I wasn't worried about flashes of light and the crackling of air that might accompany transportation to another world, but a boy's body falling from a tree was clearly something

64

to be avoided. Actually, it was all quite exciting. Then again, I've led a sheltered life.

Douglas must have been counting down because at precisely six-thirty [I say 'precisely' but of course my watch might have been wrong] he bent his legs, swung his arms back and launched himself into the air.

He landed in a puff of dust.

Douglas opened his eyes and I saw such a look of loss that it made my breath catch. He glanced at me and shook his head.

'Not enough gravity,' he whispered.

~

'Dad?' I said on the way home.

'Hmmm?'

'Can I have a bike?'

He looked at me for a moment before returning his eyes to the road.

'You can't ride a bike, Candice.'

It was true. I found it almost impossible to believe that anyone could balance on such thin strips of rubber, even though I'd seen it happen many times.

'I could learn.'

'Maybe for your birthday.'

That was no good, though I didn't say anything. I needed a bike by tomorrow. For once in my life I had somewhere I needed to be and transport was a problem.

IS FOR HAPPINESS

Dear Denille,

I understand that Americans are fond of life, liberty and the pursuit of happiness. On the off-chance that you have pursued happiness and caught it, I would welcome your advice.

My family is a mess. Ever since my baby sister died, things have become steadily worse. I could go into intimate detail about the causes of this, but I know that you are American and therefore time-poor. Consequently, I will be brief:

– *Mum: breast cancer, double mastectomy, depression.*
– *Dad: thwarted ambition, loss of wife's love (possibly), resentment of brother Brian for perceived wrongs.*
– **Rich Uncle Brian***: materially wealthy, but emotionally poor.*
– **Candice** *(me): socially inept. Add to this list a permanent sense of loss and possible guilt because of dead sister Sky and, as you can imagine, we are not the front-runners for Australian Happy Family of the Year.*

What's more, SIGNIFICANT OTHERS are faring no better. Take my English teacher, Miss Bamford. She has an eye that is not so much lazy as a complete bludger (do you have that word in America? You should. Actually, now you do, if you didn't before – an unexpected benefit of cross-cultural communication. What fun!). Children can be cruel. Her bludger eye causes much teasing from her students and I know this upsets her.

Then there is Douglas Benson From Another Dimension who is desperately unhappy at being stuck in this dimension with facsimile parents who are neither quantum physicists nor experimental musicians. I worry he is paying too much attention to a certain ravine. Sorry to be cryptic, but I dare say you get the general idea.

Now. The thing is this. Everyone wanders around, more or less aimlessly, in apparent acceptance of their fate. Douglas is the exception. He spends time jumping out of trees, but becomes dispirited when nothing happens except the occasional sprained ankle. No one is successfully pursuing happiness, with or without sprained ankles. I suspect happiness for us is not even a dot on the horizon, but has emigrated to foreign climes and left no forwarding address. Maybe it's gone to America…

This must change.

I talked things over with Earth-Pig Fish last night as is my wont when momentous things are weighing me down. Or not weighing me down, which is another matter entirely. I have to tell you, Denille, that in addition to all the other troubles afflicting me, I am totally flat-chested. My breasts have either never made an appearance or they went AWOL as soon as they did (I suspect it is the former).Earth-Pig Fish did not help in any practical way, especially with the breast dilemma, but I took her

repetitive mouth opening as a piscine method
of showing emotional support (I am up to the
letter P in my nightly reading of the dictionary.
It is an interesting letter). You see, I want to
pursue happiness. I want to catch it, grab it by
the scruff of the neck, drag it home and force it
to embrace all the people I mentioned above.

I'm just not sure how to accomplish
this. But I am determined to try.

What do you think of my plan?

Your penpal,

Candice

P.S. I suppose it isn't really a plan. A plan
should…well, plan, I imagine. The pursuit
of happiness is more of a goal or a wish. If
you think of a plan, please let me know. In
the meantime, I'll make it up as I go along.

I

I rang Rich Uncle Brian when I got home and arranged to go sailing on his yacht the following day [Sunday]. RUB was very surprised.

'I'm very surprised, Pumpkin,' he said, which gave me the initial clue.

I couldn't blame Rich Uncle Brian for being surprised. He had been trying for years to get me on board and I had always refused. I refused, not because I was being deliberately obstructive, but because boats make me sick. Literally. I do not have sea legs. I don't have sea arms. In fact, no part of my anatomy, from the smallest cell to the most major of organs, is sea anything. I throw up if someone shows me a photograph of a ship. I am suspicious of swirling water in a bathtub. You get the general idea.

'So am I, Rich Uncle Brian,' I replied. 'But it is because I need a bike.'

There was a long pause on the other end of the phone. He was probably furrowing his brows and stroking his moustache, but I wasn't in a position to say for certain. But the odds were certainly on him doing that while jingling loose change in his trouser pocket.

'Not sure of the connection between the two, Pumpkin,' he replied eventually.

'I can understand that,' I said.

There was a further long pause, which I enjoyed. I am a fan of pauses.

'Why do you want a bike, sweetie?' he asked.

'I am not at liberty to say.'

'But you can't ride a bike.'

'True. I was hoping for one with training wheels.'

'Aren't you a little old for training wheels?'

'Probably. But I am not trying to make a fashion statement.'

Rich Uncle Brian sighed. He does this a lot when we talk. Sighs and pauses. Pauses and sighs. It works for us. Then he spoke with the air of a man trying for one last time to get an answer he could understand.

'Are you saying that you will come on board the *Motherboard* if I buy you a bike with training wheels, Pumpkin? A kind of barter – one favour for another?'

That's the name of Rich Uncle Brian's yacht. *Motherboard*. I think he is exceptionally pleased with this name. He once told me he had sailed with my mother on board the *Motherboard*, and then laughed for a very long time. I laughed too, even though the joke was so weak it could barely stand. It is good to laugh at other people's jokes. It gives them pleasure and I am in favour of that.

'Correct, Rich Uncle Brian,' I replied.

'I'm happy to buy you a bike, Pumpkin. You don't have to go sailing with me to pay for it.'

I knew this was true. RUB always wanted to buy me things. It annoyed Dad and caused him to mutter. It worried Mum. It worried me, too, because I rarely wanted anything. The only person it actually pleased was Rich Uncle Brian and that was strange when you thought about it. Maybe it was best not to think about it.

'I know,' I said. 'But I also need to talk to you. In private. And it does not get much more private than a yacht in the middle of the sea. Unless we are boarded by pirates, of course, but I am prepared to take my chances.'

~

It was arranged that I would be picked up at seven in the morning. RUB promised to have a bike for me – I would need it on the Sunday evening – but I had no idea how. It was eight-thirty on a Saturday night and the shops would be closed. But Rich Uncle Brian is rich and people who have money can achieve anything.

Dad told me that, though he didn't seem especially happy when he muttered it.

I didn't eat that night. I didn't have breakfast in the morning either. It struck me there wasn't much point, since I'd probably see it again [all down my front and splattered on my shoes] a few hours later. I also asked Earth-Pig Fish's advice on dealing with water because avoiding seasickness must count as her speciality. She wasn't in a communicative mood, however, so it didn't help.

I left a note on the kitchen table telling Mum and Dad I was spending the day with RUB. There was no one around and, after all, they can both read. Then I lined my shoes with brown paper. I'd read somewhere that this is good for preventing jet lag and I thought it might work for other forms of travel. My reasoning was that if it didn't, the worst that could happen was I'd have brown paper in my shoes. This, let's be honest, was not a huge inconvenience, if I ignored the fact that I crackled slightly when I walked.

Rich Uncle Brian turned up at seven in his very big four-wheel drive. He unloaded a bike from the back of the car and wheeled it down the side of our house. It was a proper-sized bicycle and it had two big wheels at the back instead of the customary one. A grown-up tricycle, in fact.

'It's perfect, Rich Uncle Brian,' I said. 'How did you get it at such short notice?'

He rubbed the side of his nose.

'Ah, that's for me to know and you to find out,' he said, and winked.

'It is unlikely I'll find out if you don't tell me,' I replied. I wasn't a detective and Rich Uncle Brian knew this. But I winked back at him anyway.

As we walked to his car, he stopped and gazed at me.

'You are crackling when you walk,' he stated.

'Indeed,' I replied. There was no point denying it.

He scratched his nose again.

'Any reason why?'

'I have brown paper in my shoes.'

Rich Uncle Brian's mouth opened and it was obvious he was on the point of framing a question. But then he closed it again and opened the car door for me.

'Of course you have,' he muttered out of the side

of his mouth. I was glad we had both accepted this because it was clearly true and not open to any kind of interpretation.

We headed for the marina, which was where Rich Uncle Brian kept his boat. It's what marinas are for, after all. It took an hour and three minutes and we spent that time discussing my motives for going on board. Well, RUB discussed my motives. He knows about my chronic seasickness and was curious about why I would put myself through it just to talk to him [which is something I could do at the local burger bar over something deep fried and of dubious origin [see 'B Is For Birth']]. One of the advantages of being me is that no one expects sensible answers to sensible questions, so he didn't make much progress. But it passed the time.

Even I have to admit that RUB's yacht is beautiful. It is white. And long. And luxurious. It has *Motherboard* written in cursive script on the prow [that's the front of the boat – I think I mentioned I am up to P in the dictionary] and there are all sorts of amenities on board. Two large bedrooms with shiny manchester and DVD players built in to the ceilings. A spa, in case RUB wanted more water than the ocean provided. On deck, there were tall masts with winches, ropes and stainless steel cranks for purposes that remained a mystery to me.

Rich Uncle Brian was dressed all in white and sported a peaked cap with *Motherboard* written in cursive characters identical to the letters on the side of the yacht. He wore pure white deck shoes, which I threw up on as soon as I set foot on the gangplank.

'Sorry, Rich Uncle Brian,' I said.

He looked down at what appeared to be diced carrots on his previously pristine [the letter P is fabulous!] shoes and smiled crookedly.

'Love is never having to say you're sorry, Pumpkin,' he said.

'I have no idea what that means,' I replied.

'Neither do I,' he replied.

I gestured towards his shoes.

'I haven't eaten carrots in...' I did some mental maths. 'Well, never, actually. I'm not sure that is mine.'

'Seems to be mine now,' he added, and stroked his moustache. 'Not a problem, Pumpkin. A little water clears us of this deed.'

'That's Lady Macbeth,' I said. 'You are rich, Rich Uncle Brian, and a computer expert. How do you know Shakespeare?' I would have been interested in his reply, but unfortunately I threw up again and that put a cap on the conversation. If this was how my body responded to being on the gangplank [and clearly it was], I was concerned about how I would react when

I finally got on deck. If water was going to clear us of these deeds, then it was just as well there was a whole ocean out there.

Within two hours we were surrounded by nothing, unless we counted the sea as something, which it obviously was. I managed to get rid of everything that had been in my stomach for the last three months, which raised interesting questions about biology. Surely I must have digested *something* in a quarter of a year? RUB gave me a bucket which he emptied over the side at regular intervals. I worried about the fish out there.

In the short intervals between vomiting, I got straight to the point.

'Rich Uncle Brian,' I said. 'There is a schism between you and my dad.' [I hadn't got to S in the dictionary yet, but was looking forward to it.] 'This is a great shame and there must be a way to mend that breaaaaach.' I meant to say 'breach' but spread its syllable somewhat. I spread quite a bit of everything actually. Rich Uncle Brian hosed down the deck and considered his response.

'Do we really want to go there, Pumpkin?' he said finally.

'Yes,' I said, wiping my mouth.

RUB sat opposite me and stroked his moustache,

but kept his hand away from his pocket. I was pleased about this. It was obvious he was thinking carefully, weighing words, deciding exactly what he could or couldn't say about my father. I decided to help him out.

'I know that Dad thinks you stole his ideas and that you believe you didn't,' I said. 'I do not make judgements, but it is obvious Dad is jealous of your success and wealth. And it is also obvious you have more money than is seemly. Wouldn't the simplest solution be if you gave him a whopping pile of cash and then everyone would be happy?'

This was the longest speech I had made in, possibly, years. Not so much in terms of words [though I couldn't remember the last time I had strung so many together], but certainly as far as time was concerned. I have transcribed it as best I can remember, but it actually took ten minutes to get the words out as I was throwing up into a bucket for most of that time. Rich Uncle Brian cleaned up with a rueful expression, and a mop that was getting smellier by the second.

'I've tried, Pumpkin,' he said. 'I've tried. It's not that simple, unfortunately.'

Twelve years is not a huge number to accumulate and call it a life, but even so, I wouldn't mind a dollar for every time I'd heard that things are not that simple. I wouldn't be able to buy a yacht, but I could afford my own tricycle. I waited for RUB to continue. It was obvious he was squirming on the horns of a dilemma.

'I offered your dad half of my income from that patent,' he said. 'He turned me down. What he wanted was the legal acknowledgement that he co-wrote it, as well as half the royalties. I couldn't accept that. He didn't write it. I did. The money? Hey, he was welcome to that. But I wouldn't lie about the authorship. I couldn't, Pumpkin. I simply couldn't.'

He scratched his nose and bent his head towards the contents of my sick bucket, which is indicative of how desperate he was to avoid my eyes. I'd seen inside that bucket from close range, and it wasn't pretty.

'So you don't talk to each other because of a signature, or lack thereof, on a piece of paper?'

'Sounds silly when it's put like that, but yes. That's about the sum of it.'

I didn't say much for the rest of the trip. I needed to chew over the insights that Rich Uncle Brian had provided. As well as the remains of diced carrots stuck between my teeth. But just as we were coming into port, I gave it one more go.

'Rich Uncle Brian?' I said.

'Hmmm?'

'Do you still love your brother?'

While considering this question he plonked the

empty bucket in front of me, did things with stainless steel cranks, threw ropes overboard and tied them to metal posts. The yacht bobbed gently in the swell and ropes creaked. Or maybe that was my stomach. Finally, he sat down, took off his cap and wiped sweat from his face. There were tears in his eyes.

'I do, Pumpkin. I surely do.'

'And would you do anything to mend that breach?'

'Of course. Apart from acknowledging he was the co-author of my program. That's the only thing I cannot do.' He gave a tired smile. 'And yet that's the only thing your father wants. It's an impossible situation, Pumpkin.'

I wasn't sure. A plan was forming in my mind. It wasn't foolproof. It wasn't ironclad. It wasn't even fully formed. More of a proto-plan, really. But it might work. I was so excited by the possibilities I didn't even throw up as we went down the gangplank. And I didn't feel like talking as Rich Uncle Brian drove me home. He tried, though.

'Did you enjoy your trip?' he asked.

I tore my attention away from the logistical problems involved in my plan and gave his question some consideration. I knew it would be insensitive to tell the truth. A simple 'Yes' – a white lie – was the required response, and I opened my mouth to do just that.

'It was disgusting, Rich Uncle Brian,' I said.

His mouth turned downwards and I instantly felt bad.

'But I did enjoy our talk,' I added. Sometimes it is good to throw in two truths if one can compensate for the other.

'Tell me, Pumpkin,' he said a minute later. 'Does your dad ever mention me? You asked if I still loved him. Do you think there's a chance he still loves me?'

'No,' I said. 'Whenever your name is mentioned his mouth twists up and he mutters darkly.'

I couldn't think of another truth to make up for that one.

IS FOR JOKE-SHOP JUNK

Rich Uncle Brian dropped me home at five o'clock. There was no sign of Mum. Her bedroom curtains were closed and the door was shut. I went around the side of the house and stood in the doorway of Dad's shed. He had his headphones on and his computer lights were flashing. He didn't notice me, but that's not exactly news. I was able to see part of the screen as his fingers flashed over the keys. The screen was mainly dark, apart from a series of symbols that scrolled down the page. His foot tapped relentlessly.

It was a mystery.

Dad was a mystery.

I wheeled my tricycle to the front yard and through the gate. RUB had left a bike helmet draped over the handlebars. I put it on and tightened the chinstrap. Then I sat on the saddle, which was long, pointed and designed to wedge itself firmly up my bottom.

I fell off on the first bend.

I believe this is actually a matter for considerable pride. The tricycle was VERY stable. The back wheels were wide and, according to Douglas Benson From Another Dimension [whom I told the story to later], the trike should have remained upright in a cyclone. Douglas said it was contrary to the laws of physics to fall off that tricycle and I believe him. Douglas knows his physics. Nonetheless, no matter how offensive to science, I fell off and scraped my leg bloody on the asphalt. It was still more pleasant than being on Rich Uncle Brian's yacht.

Apart from that, I made it to my destination with no further mishaps. I hid the bike under a tree, although it was unlikely that anyone would happen to pass by and steal it. Then again, I reminded myself, it was exceptionally unlikely that anyone would fall off a tricycle, so I wasn't prepared to take chances. I walked the rest of the way.

Douglas's ravine was as pretty as ever. Well, I imagined it was as pretty as ever because I kept a healthy distance from the edge. It was six-fifteen, so I sat under a gum tree and kept a lookout. I was a coiled spring, ready to bounce into action should the situation require. But fifteen minutes passed. And then twenty [which wasn't surprising, considering the nature of time] and Douglas didn't show. I became an uncoiled spring at six-forty-five and walked back to my bike. I didn't fall off once on my way home, which was a relief to both me and the laws of physics.

~

I ruminated and cogitated throughout school on Monday. Probably more ruminating than cogitating, but certainly a considerable amount of both. One of the advantages of no one talking to me is that there is plenty of time for uninterrupted r and c.

This is the way my thoughts went:

Mum and Dad were miserable together, but were they miserable because they were together or would they be miserable in isolation? Dad might be miserable because Mum was always locked in her room being miserable, but he might also be miserable because of the rift between himself and Rich Uncle Brian, which has nothing to do with Mum per se [though she would be more prone to being miserable with the miserable rift between her husband and her brother-in-law, and therefore more likely to be less miserable if that miserable rift was healed]. But maybe Dad was miserable not because of the rift, but because Rich Uncle Brian was the sole author of the patent, in which case he [Dad] would remain miserable regardless of rifts, healed or otherwise. And maybe Mum was miserable because of her breast cancer and the death of her daughter, in which case there would be nothing I could do, since I cannot raise the dead nor restore breasts once they have been removed, though maybe I could do something about giving her a reason to feel optimistic, so healing the rift might be a step in the right direction after all. And maybe Rich Uncle Brian was miserable about something other than the rift, so healing it might not restore him to the heights of happiness. And Douglas. He was miserable because he can't get back to his world, which [to be honest] I'm not convinced exists anyway, so getting him back there might prove to be an impossibility, and even if it is all true then how could I do that when I don't even know what a tesseract is, let alone pea brains and all the other things necessary to make the journey a success [assuming it's possible]?

I was confused. It was no wonder no one talked to me. I wouldn't talk to me if I had a choice.

I decided I would start with a more straightforward task. Miss Bamford's eye. As far as I could determine, this was a simple problem with a simple solution.

I stopped at the joke shop on my way home from school [actually, it calls itself a party-hire shop, but I'm not sure I would go to a party with a whoopee cushion and a resin model of dog poo. Then again, I don't go to parties, so I'm not an expert]. I invested twenty-four dollars of pocket money. When I got home I rang Douglas Benson From Another Dimension and asked him to do some internet research for me and to bring the information to school the following day. I could have asked Dad, but I didn't want to interrupt his strange-symbol scrolling. Mum was in bed again, so I heated leftovers in the microwave and ate by myself.

By the time I had finished it was close to six o'clock, so I hopped on my bike [actually, I edged onto my bike – that saddle was like a razor blade] and headed off to the ravine again. There was more traffic, it being Monday, but I avoided getting killed, which would have put a dampener on my day. Douglas didn't put in an appearance for the second day running and I was pleased. Although it was likely I'd be riding to that ravine for the foreseeable future, I was happy if the only thing I experienced was a sore bottom rather than the sight of a friend plummeting to certain death [or an alternative universe, whichever came first]. It was a tired Candice Phee who crawled into bed at nine-thirty, having fed Earth-Pig Fish who was not in the mood for constructive conversation. But it was also a contented Candice Phee, because she had plans to improve the general state of happiness in the world. True, it would make only a few people happy, but it was a start.

The rest of the world would have to wait.

~

The staff room was a hive of activity on Tuesday morning. There was laughter coming from within and no one heard me knocking. I had to hammer three times before someone opened the door. I wondered what was going on. Nearly all the teachers I know are sombre people in the classroom, discouraging jokes and generally appearing to have ruled laughter entirely out of their lives.

Mr Gemmola, my Maths teacher, opened the door. His broad smile vanished when he saw me. Maybe there was something about the close proximity of students that altered a teacher's behaviour, like iron filings close to a magnet.

'Good morning, Miss Phee,' he said in sepulchral tones [I have reached S in the dictionary]. 'What can I do for you?'

'You could smile, Mr Gemmola,' I replied. 'It suits you.'

My honesty puzzles many people, teachers included. He didn't reply, but cocked his head to one side.

'Alternatively,' I continued, 'you could ask Miss Bamford if she would be willing to see me.'

She was and she did. We went to a classroom and she sat behind her desk. She laced her fingers together and peered at me over half-moon specs. Well, one eye peered at me; the other had its own agenda. She would have been better off with a monocle. I organised my thoughts. This was going to be a delicate conversation in which tact and diplomacy was required. Luckily, I had considered this as I lay in bed the previous night. I had rehearsed not just my tactics, but also the exact words I would use. I took a deep breath.

'You know your weird eye, Miss Bamford?' I started. 'How it spins out of control like a punctured balloon?'

She didn't say anything, which I took as confirmation I'd made a positive start.

'Douglas Benson From Another Dimension says it's so hyperactive it should be on Ritalin,' I added. 'But that is not the issue. I suspect, Miss Bamford, that you are aware of the cruel remarks made about your peripatetic eyeball.'

Miss Bamford raised a hand in the stop position. I stopped because that was only polite.

'Candice?' she said. 'Do you mind if I ask you a question?'

'Not at all, Miss Bamford,' I replied. 'Ask two, if the urge is irresistible.'

'I'm curious. You rarely say anything in class – or out of it, if the rumours are to be believed – yet, when you do talk, your vocabulary is remarkable for a twelve-year-old. "Peripatetic" for example. Can you explain?'

'Yes,' I said. 'Certainly.'

There was a long pause. I felt the urge to hum, but kept control. Miss Bamford fixed me with a quizzical eye. The other examined a pinboard at the back of the classroom.

'Well?' she said finally.

'Oh. I see. Well, peripatetic means something that wanders or travels a lot. It…'

'No, no, Candice.' Miss Bamford sighed. She sounded like Rich Uncle Brian. 'I know what the word means. I want to know how *you* know what it means.'

Things were becoming clearer. 'I read the dictionary, Miss Bamford,' I replied. 'Every night. It is my favourite book. At the moment I am up to the letter S, which is stupendous. It sets a very high standard which frankly I suspect T will not be able to match. But one should not pre-judge.'

Miss Bamford rubbed at her forehead.

'I imagine, Candice,' she said, 'that reading the dictionary would increase your raw vocabulary, but it doesn't explain how you *use* the words you pick up. Surely you must read other things?'

'You are sagacious, Miss Bamford,' I replied, partly to confirm the rich treasure trove that is the letter S. 'I also read Dickens.'

'Charles Dickens?'

'The same.'

'Any other writers?'

'No. Dickens is sufficient. I have his complete works and read them in alphabetical order. I am currently up to *Dombey and Sons*. It is my second cycle through his lifework.'

Miss Bamford made a little resting place for her chin with interlaced fingers. Then she cleared her throat.

'Dickens is a wonderful writer, Candice,' she said. 'But don't you think you should read other writers occasionally?'

It was clear that Miss Bamford was not limiting herself to the one question she had requested. Or, indeed, the two I had counter-offered. But I felt it would be churlish to point this out.

'No,' I said.

'Isn't he a little out of date?' she continued. 'Perhaps, for modern tastes, rather too...old?'

'He would be two hundred years of age,' I replied. 'Which would certainly be too old for modern tastes.

But he is dead. And that makes a huge difference. Particularly, I imagine, to him.'

Miss Bamford's mouth twitched and I felt confident she was about to ask yet another question about my reading habits. But then she gave a little wave of her hand as if giving up the whole conversation as a bad job.

'You were saying about my eye,' she whispered.

'Ah, yes,' I replied. 'It seems to me, Miss Bamford, that there is a simple solution to your ocular problem. What is more, I have this solution in my school bag and would ask that you consider it seriously.' I rummaged around in my backpack, found the large paper bag and pushed it across the desk. She opened the top and peered inside. I waited for her reaction and didn't have to wait long.

'A hook, a plastic sword and a rubber parrot,' she said. 'This is very kind of you, Candice, but it raises more questions, I think, than it answers.'

'I catch your drift,' I replied. 'The point is, Miss Bamford, that I bought these items as a pirate's job lot. I am not suggesting you attach the hook or pin the parrot to your shoulder, though that would be a personal choice and I wouldn't stand in your way. It is the eye patch that I want to bring to your attention. You see, if you put it on, then no one could see your wandering eye. This would, at a stroke, reduce the teasing you currently endure. Plus, it would lend you a certain air. Sinister perhaps, or even romantic. It would establish an aura of mystery. And who would dare tease a sinister, romantic, mysterious one-eyed teacher sporting a black eye patch? Count me out, for one.'

I said earlier that teachers leave their senses of humour in the staff room. Well, it only goes to show one should never make generalisations [which is in itself a generalisation I should not have made] because Miss Bamford did a curious thing. She removed her specs and placed them on the desk. Then she lowered her head so it rested next to them. Her shoulders shook, almost imperceptibly at first, but then with increasing vigour. It was as if she were impersonating an earthquake. For a moment I thought she was crying, possibly out of gratitude that I had solved her problem. I believe that happens. But then I heard the distinct peals of what was obviously laughter. She lifted her head and her eyes were red and streaming with tears. Miss Bamford howled. Then she howled some more. I waited patiently. There is little point, in my experience, attempting to converse with someone who is howling like a hyena. So I folded my arms and weathered the storm.

It took time for Miss Bamford to calm down. When she did, she fixed me with her one good eye.

'Thank you, Candice,' she said, though her voice was weak. 'You have made my day.'

'You could dye it a different colour if black does not suit,' I said, 'though I believe black would lend gravitas.'

Her mouth twitched and I thought she was going to start laughing again. But she maintained control. My job here was done and I rose to go.

'Enjoy,' I said at the door, and she gave a small gurgle followed by a muffled snigger. I was almost through when she stopped me.

'Candice?' she said. I turned. 'Where is your assignment? The alphabet recount? It is not like you to be late.'

'Sorry, Miss,' I replied. 'I'm up to J, but it's taking longer than I thought.'

'I'm looking forward to reading it.'

'I'm looking forward to finishing it.'

~

Jambalaya is a Louisiana Creole dish of Spanish and French influence, popular in the French Quarter of New Orleans. So said the internet page printouts that Douglas Benson From Another Dimension gave me at recess, and I have no reason to doubt them.

Some explanation is called for.

I have already mentioned that Mum was not always depressed. Before Sky died she was active, optimistic and full of plans. I remember one conversation, though I cannot remember when or where it happened. The only image I can bring to mind is sitting in a restaurant. Dad wasn't there and nor was Sky, though I'm sure this was after her birth and certainly before her death. Mum was leaning over the table and her face was bright, alive with emotion.

'One day, Pumpkin,' she said. 'One day we will all go to the United States and visit New Orleans. It is a place I *must* see before I die.'

'What's there, Mummy?'

She leaned back and a dreamy expression spread across her face.

'All kinds of things, Pumpkin. You walk through the French Quarter and see amazing railings, beautiful, scrolled ironwork everywhere. And the streets…they are full of people, most talking French, and the music, Pumpkin, the music…from every shopfront, from every balcony, jazz musicians play. On each street corner someone plays a saxophone or a guitar or a trumpet. We'll eat jambalaya and gumbo and listen to jazz and watch people dance in the streets, surrounded by French accents, surrounded by music…'

Nothing else remains of that memory except her expression. Transported into another place, she was happy. New Orleans was never mentioned after that.

Like everything else, it shrivelled and died. But at least I remember.

~

During lunchtime I sat in my special chair in the library and made a shopping list. Douglas was scouring the bookshelves for information on gravity, so I had time and space. I would need chicken, smoked sausage, onions, capsicums, tomatoes, prawns, chicken stock and rice [though I thought we already had rice].

What with shopping, tricycling to the ravine and cooking, it promised to be a busy and, hopefully, productive evening. I was worried though. Apart from an egg [which turned out disastrously] I had never cooked anything in my life. I scanned the recipe. Unfortunately, microwave ovens did not feature anywhere.

There are people, I am told, who enjoy cooking, who do it every night. They slice and dice, they top and tail, they braise and stew, they poach and steam, all the time laughing like idiots in a delirium of happiness.

I didn't laugh, I couldn't say I was entirely happy, but I was certainly an idiot.

The recipe called for me to slice the capsicums, but I took no chances and sliced my fingers as well. This slowed me down as every ten seconds I had to get a new bandaid and try to stem the flow of blood. Even so, by the time I had the ingredients ready ['prepped' according to the recipe Douglas had given me] the kitchen was the scene of a nasty traffic accident involving multiple amputations. I mopped the floor and wiped down surfaces, which was difficult with fingers like bandaid-covered sausages. Finally, though, the big pot was simmering on the stove. I threw in the rice and covered it, turning the flame low. The jambalaya had to cook for over an hour, which gave me time to get to Douglas's ravine and back again.

Once again, it was a wasted journey, though I don't want to imply that Douglas jumping off a cliff would have been a constructive use of time. Anyway, I arrived home with sore hands and a sore bum and got back to work. There were one or two things that needed to be done to create the right atmosphere. I was concerned that the cooking smells would have woken Mum and prompted her to investigate, but I needn't have worried. No one, as far as I could tell, had been in the kitchen. I bustled around, making a few final touches, and then trotted off to Dad's shed.

I stood for a moment in the doorway, watching the lights flash and the symbols scroll down the page, before I tapped him on the shoulder. He turned and lifted one headphone away from an ear.

'Dad,' I said. 'I have made dinner.'

He removed his headphones entirely and swivelled in his chair to face me. It was difficult to read his expression, but 'puzzled' would certainly come close.

'You've done what?' he said.

I didn't think I had been vague, but obviously I needed to explain.

'I've made dinner,' I said.

'Why?'

'So we could eat it.'

'But I've eaten. Spaghetti and meatballs. I left a covered plate for you in the microwave.'

'Thanks. I'll put it in the fridge. Or maybe the bin. The food, not the microwave. Then you'll eat my food.'

'Why?'

The way this conversation was going, we'd be here at eleven o'clock with the jambalaya a blackened mess stuck to the bottom of the pan. I decided I would have to confide in him.

'I've cooked a special meal for Mum,' I said. 'To cheer her up. I bought all the ingredients and spent three hours cooking her favourite dish.' [I exaggerated slightly, but the situation called for it.] 'I thought it would be nice if, for once, we ate together as a family. Please, Dad? Your computer isn't going anywhere.' *As opposed to this family, which is disappearing down the toilet*, I thought. I was going to keep this to myself, but then reconsidered. 'As opposed to this family, which is disappearing down the toilet,' I added.

'Your Mum's in bed,' said Dad. 'Does she know about this?'

'Not exactly,' I replied.

'Not exactly?'

'Well, not even not approximately,' I confessed. 'She has no idea. But I'm just about to wake her. It would be helpful if I could say we are both waiting around the dinner table.'

'We have a dinner table?'

'It is square, made of wood and has chairs around it.'

Dad pretended to think things over, but we both knew he didn't have a choice. He sighed, clicked something on his computer and put the headphones on the desk. He got to his feet with the air of someone wearied by life and burdened by worries. Dad is tall, thin and permanently stooped, probably from spending his entire life leaning forward and peering at a computer screen. If he had a hooked nose he'd look *exactly* like a vulture, but he doesn't, so he doesn't.

'I hope you can wake your Mum,' he said. 'She's been very tired recently.'

'I'll manage,' I said. 'Now, if you could just put this string of onions around your neck…'

'I'm sorry?'

'No need to apologise.'

'A string of onions?'

'Yes. And this beret, preferably at a jaunty angle. Plus, it would be helpful if you could manage the majority of the dinner conversation in French.'

'I'm sorry?'

'There you go again. Here is a list of French phrases, with indications of correct pronunciation. This should help you deal with most topics of conversation. Of course, it goes without saying that these should be accompanied with shrugs of the shoulder and the occasional "*Sacrebleu*".'

Dad seemed on the verge of making a remark [possibly to apologise once more], but thought better of it. He put the string of onions round his neck [do you have any idea how difficult it is to thread onions together?] and glanced at the list I'd prepared at lunchtime with the help of the library English–French dictionary. I'd enjoyed that dictionary. It wasn't as easy to understand as the English one, but much more romantic. Dad loped off to sit at the dinner table. I stirred the jambalaya, put the stereo on low and knocked on Mum's bedroom door.

It took time to rouse her, but eventually she sat up in bed with tousled hair and a matching expression.

'What is it, Pumpkin?' she said.

'*Il est* dinner-time, *je pense*,' I replied. I'd looked up the French for 'dinner', but had forgotten it.

['*Déjeuner*'? Or was that lunch?] I had to accept that fluent French was beyond Dad and Mum and me, and that the occasional English word would have to substitute.

'I'm sorry?' she replied.

I had never received so many apologies in such a short time.

'I've made dinner,' I said. 'Dad is sitting at the table and all we need is you. I cooked jambalaya. *Votre* favourite.' I strung out the last syllable of 'favourite' so it would sound French, but I think it came out more like Mexican.

Mum, obviously puzzled, swung her legs out of bed and pulled on her dressing gown. It was not formal wear, but I wasn't going to push my luck. I decided against giving her a beret on the grounds that there would be a clash of styles. She put a hand against her eyes and shuffled out the door.

Dad cut a dashing figure with his string of onions and the beret. Mum took one look at him and stifled a laugh.

'What is going on?' she asked.

'A French-themed *déjeuner*,' I said, putting on my own beret and necklace of onions. Actually, they were incredibly powerful. The onions, not the berets. I worried that Dad and I would spend the evening crying softly into our jambalaya, but it was worth the risk. I lit candles and turned up the volume on the stereo. A plaintive saxophone swirled through the air. Well, actually it didn't. That could only happen in a Harry Potter movie. The *sound* of a plaintive saxophone swirled through the air.

'What have you done to your hands?' asked Mum.

'The latest in oven gloves,' I replied. I opened a bottle of wine and poured a glass for Mum and Dad. I'd found the wine at the back of the fridge. Once upon a time my parents would sit in the back garden and share a bottle. That was so long ago I wasn't sure it was a genuine memory. I worried the wine might be off. I had an image of Mum and Dad kneeling side by side and retching down the same toilet, but then I thought if anything was going to do that it would be my cooking.

'But before we eat,' I said, '*voulez-vous dance avec moi, Papa?*'

'I'm sorry?' said Dad.

'That has been established. Would you like to dance with me?'

'I can't dance,' he said with the conviction of a career computer geek.

'Then now is the time to learn.' I stood and held out my arms. Mum giggled. For a moment I couldn't place the sound because it was so unfamiliar. I hadn't heard her laugh for years. Dad got to his feet. Even he was smiling. He took my arms and we shuffled around the floor for a minute. My head was buried in his stomach. In a world's worst dancer competition, it would have been a close run thing whether he or I would have scored first place. Four left feet moved without any idea of timing.

'Giant steps, Dad?' I asked.

He groaned. When I was little I used to stand on his feet and he'd lurch around while I screamed with laughter. I was heavier now, but I'm not what you would call a porker. I slipped off my shoes, stood on his insteps and we swayed drunkenly around the dining room. At least we had reduced the left feet by fifty percent. Mum laughed and clapped as the song finished and we juddered to a halt.

'*Merci bien*,' I said.

'I'm sorry?' said Dad.

'*Papa! Parle Francais!*'

'Oh, yes.' He dug the piece of paper I gave him out of his pocket and looked it over. His brow scrunched up in concentration.

'*Votre grenouille a mangé mon déjeuner*,' he said.

'*Bien sur*,' I replied.

'What does that mean anyway?' Dad said.

'"Your frog has eaten my dinner." Or it might be lunch. A useful phrase, I'm sure you will agree.'

Mum's giggles increased to the extent that she was choking. I turned towards her, but she waved me away with a hand.

'Enough,' I said. 'It is time for dinner. *Asseyez, s'il vous plait.*' To assist them with comprehension, I sat at the table and indicated they should do the same.

The jambalaya looked like the recent contents of the bucket on Rich Uncle Brian's yacht. It didn't smell quite as bad, however, so I served it up. I placed brimming plates in front of Mum and Dad with what I hoped was panache [another French word!]. Dad gazed at the food as if confronted with roadkill. He poked the jambalaya with a fork, possibly to establish if it was still alive.

'What's in it, Candice?' he asked.

'Chicken, smoked sausage, onions, capsicums, tomatoes, prawns, chicken stock and rice,' I replied. 'Though not necessarily in that order.'

'You didn't peel the prawns before cooking them?'

'The recipe said to de-vein them, but I am not skilled at micro-cosmetic surgery, so I didn't. Should they be peeled?'

'It's lovely, Pumpkin,' said Mum. She took a mouthful and chewed slowly. One of *her* veins stood out on her forehead. 'Such an unusual taste! Where's your plate?'

'After all that cooking, I'm not hungry,' I said.

I think Dad mumbled something about 'wise', but I could be mistaken. I put another jazz CD on the player and watched them eat. It was strange, but when they finished there seemed to be more on their plates than I'd served in the first place.

'Delicious,' said Mum.

'Beautiful,' said Dad.

'What made you choose this dish, Pumpkin?' asked Mum.

'New Orleans,' I said. 'I remembered you said you wanted to see it before you died. The jazz, the French Quarter, the jambalaya and the gumbo, the saxophones on street corners. Do you remember?'

Mum's eyes clouded and a smile played around her lips.

'I'd almost forgotten,' she said. 'Yes. The dreams. The dreams I had when I was young.'

'It wasn't when you were young,' I replied. 'It was only a few years back.'

'Thanks,' she said.

'Anyway,' I continued, 'they don't have to remain dreams.'

'You are kind, Pumpkin,' said Mum. 'And I am very proud of you. Thank you.'

'French,' I said.

'*Merci*,' she said.

I washed the dishes, and when I came back into the dining room, I discovered a small miracle. Mum and Dad were dancing. He had his arms around her waist and they swayed gently to a slow rhythm. Her head was pressed against his chest. Their eyes were closed, but their lips were smiling. I watched for a few moments and then Mum opened her eyes and looked straight at me. Her eyes were smiling as well.

IS FOR LAUGHTER

Dear Denille,

I have learned a lesson.

I learned it from Miss Bamford, my English teacher, which, on the face of it, is not surprising. But I am not talking about spelling, punctuation and grammatical structure. I am talking about language, laughter and life. Let me tell you what happened...

Actually, I won't, if it's all the same to you. I have just written it down for an English assignment and I am tired and can't face repeating myself. So I'll cut to the chase (you

*won't need reminding that I am making
considerable efforts with American idioms).
I made people laugh today and it was wonderful.
I didn't intend to. In fact, it wasn't part of
my thinking at all. All I wanted was to make
the people in my life a little happier, but for
some reason they found my actions funny.*

I am NOT, *Denille, a funny person
by nature.*

I cannot tell jokes.

*I would not win any talent contests for
humour. Actually, I wouldn't win any
talent contests for anything.*

*Let me give you an example of how my
mind works when it comes to humour. Miss
Bamford, my English teacher, she of the
independently gyrating eyeball, once quoted
something to my class. We were doing silent
reading and had to bring along our own books
(I brought my dictionary) and she said that
someone (an American, I believe) had remarked
that 'outside of a dog, a book is a man's best
friend. Inside a dog, it's too dark to read.' She
laughed in an uproarious fashion. I understood
how the joke operates (it's the two meanings
of the word 'outside' – literally on the outside*

of something and 'apart from' or 'excluding').
But some things about the joke bothered me.
I would have put my hand up to ask her, but
that would have taken too long, so I did what
I always do under these circumstances. I ripped
out a sheet of paper and began to write.

~

Dear Miss Bamford, I understand the joke
and think it is a clever play on words, but
I have a few questions. How did someone
get inside a dog in the first place? It seems a
physical impossibility. Furthermore, if one
accepts that it is possible (which I doubt) then
the circumstances of the ingestion would be
important. Was the person intending to enter
the dog or was it against that person's will? If
the latter, then it is unlikely that the person
would a) be carrying a book and b) have the
composure to read once he or she was inside
the dog (presumably within the stomach)?
Even I, who loves reading, would be looking
for escape, rather than curling up for a good
read. If, on the other hand, the person entered
the dog willingly, book in hand, then we
would reasonably expect them to have the
foresight to be carrying a torch or one of those

battery-operated lights that clip on the page.

I know you will accuse me of being too literal, but I can't stop questions from entering my mind where they worry away at me until answered satisfactorily.

Yours,

Candice Phee

~

Of course, she only laughed when she read it.

I digress, but only slightly.

You see, it appears I can make people laugh without intending to. I gave my teacher an eye patch to solve the out-of-control eyeball problem. She laughed. I tried to recreate New Orleans in our dining room for my mother. She laughed. Laughter is good. Laughter is wonderful. I often don't understand where it comes from, but I like the effect it produces.

My family does not have enough laughter in it. All the laughter evaporated when my sister died.

Anyway, I don't know how I make people laugh, but I want to continue doing it.

The thing is, although laughter might be the best medicine, it cannot cure the cancer that took my mother's breasts, it cannot cure sudden infant death syndrome, it cannot cure depression and it cannot cure the bitterness within two brothers' hearts. It cannot move us back in time to when all was well.

I don't know how to do these things, but I know I must try. The laughter will be a bonus.

There is another problem that has been weighing heavily with me recently and it concerns another friend I have already referred to. Earth-Pig Fish. You may remember that, in a previous letter, I told you my concerns regarding her religious temperament and how she might regard me as a deity on account of my occasional seemingly mystical appearances where wonders are performed (like fish food on the surface of the water – a sort of fishy manna). I do not want to be a god to Earth-Pig Fish. I want to be her friend. What if she is praying to me to grant her immortality? I cannot do that (mind you, neither can God, apparently, but I'd feel guilty, whereas He, it seems, doesn't). What if she believes that if she does die, she will be brought, in a fanfare of heavenly trumpets, to my bosom and live in eternal bliss when in actual fact she's almost certainly destined to be flushed down the toilet?

I want Earth-Pig Fish to become an atheist.
I do not know how to do this.

It occurs to me I could remove myself from
her consciousness by wrapping her bowl in black
plastic, but this would also condemn her to
darkness (and would she then interpret that as a
form of Hell for sins unknowingly committed?)
So I have been considering developing an auto-
matic feeding system whereby her granules are
dispensed daily but without human involvement.
I am not mechanically minded, but I suspect
Douglas Benson From Another Dimension, who
is a scientist, might help. Of course, this raises
another problem. How can I be her friend if
she doesn't know I exist? Maybe I could be
her friend regardless – invisible, but doing the
right thing by her, looking out for her from
a distance, catering for her every need and
ensuring her world is comfortable and secure.

The trouble is, that sounds like I am setting
myself up as a god, which brings me full circle.

Americans know about religion, I have been
assured, so I welcome your theological insights.

Your penpal,
Candice

IS FOR MOURNING

Today is Friday, 14 June.

I will be thirteen on Sunday. I am looking forward to that. Twelve seems very young, whereas thirteen carries with it the implication that you have completed your apprenticeship as a child and can do teenagery-type things without appearing a fraud. Not that I think I will be able to do teenagery-type things.

Jen Marshall can.

Remember Jen Marshall? [see 'A Is For Assignment'].

She has a tattoo.

She has a pierced belly button.

She has eye make-up.

She has love bites.

She has in-your-face boobs.

She has an iPhone in one hand and an iPod in the other.

She is permanently bored.

It is rumoured she drinks a lot of cider.

All the girls in my class want to be just like her.

I, meanwhile, have a flat chest and a pernickety pencil case.

Not only does no one want to be *just* like me, no one wants to be *anything* like me. And who can blame them?

A few years ago, I used to dread my birthday. Mum and Dad would go to considerable effort to make it a happy occasion. There would be streamers around the house and a cake with candles. Nicely wrapped presents. But there were always two dark and brooding clouds looming over us. One was Rich Uncle Brian, even though he doesn't *look* much like a cloud, dark, brooding or otherwise. Mum and Dad never had much money, but they would buy lovely gifts for my birthday – pens, dictionaries, sensible shoes, fluffy socks. I did enjoy unwrapping them. Rich Uncle Brian has loads of money and bought me an expensive sound system [that I never used] or a plasma TV [that I never plugged in] or glittering jewellery [that I never wore].

Dad would gaze from his present [nice gel pens] to Rich Uncle Brian's present [a limited edition solid gold Cartier fountain pen] and his face would sag, like he was carrying two kilos of potatoes in it. He'd smile, but it came out crooked. Within minutes, he would wander back to his shed, muttering darkly. My birthday would effectively be over. Two years ago, however, I took Rich Uncle Brian to one side and we had a frank conversation.

'I do not want you to buy me any more birthday presents, Rich Uncle Brian.'

His face sagged. That probably wasn't his fault. There must be a dominant gene responsible for face-sagging that runs in the male line of the family.

'Why ever not, Pumpkin?'

'Because you are a dark and brooding cloud, Rich Uncle Brian,' I said. 'I speak metaphorically. No offence.'

He sighed and gazed at me with eyes of liquidy sadness. He stroked his moustache. He jingled coins in his pocket. I felt the need to clarify.

'I'm a gel pen kind of girl, Rich Uncle Brian, rather than a solid gold Cartier fountain pen kind of girl. Your presents are too expensive.'

'I can afford them.'

'But I can't afford to receive them.'

'You want me to buy you gel pens?'

'No. Dad buys me gel pens. It's what he does.'

'So what then?' He spread his arms wide. 'I can't not buy you anything, Pumpkin. You're my only niece and I love you.'

I considered his point and deemed it fair.

'Give money to charity on my behalf,' I said. 'There are starving children all over the world. Save lives, Rich Uncle Brian, rather than giving me things I don't want and can't use. That would be the best present.'

There was some argument. RUB likes things you can see and touch and hear and smell. Preferably expensive things. He wasn't impressed with the idea of saving the lives of people he had never met. You couldn't see, touch, hear or smell that kind of present. But I got my way. Now I receive regular reports on irrigation projects in Africa, educational programs in Asia and improved health outcomes in remote indigenous communities. They are better than gel pens and that is saying a lot.

So. One dark and brooding cloud dissolved away, but another remains.

My sister Sky died on the fifteenth of June. Tomorrow is the anniversary of her death. She would have been seven.

No one has ever discussed this, no one has drawn

up a plan or a schedule, but over the years, a routine has been established for the anniversary of Sky's death. On the Saturday closest to the date [and tomorrow coincides exactly] we dress in our best sombre clothes. We drive to the cemetery. We spend a few hours at her gravestone. If it is sunny, we spread out a blanket on the grass. If it is raining, we take camping chairs and umbrellas. Dad paces back and forth, back and forth, and doesn't say anything. Mum cries, normally without making a sound. I watch Mum and Dad, go for a walk and wait for time to pass. It always does. Eventually. Then we drive home and Mum retreats to her room, Dad retreats to his shed and I retreat to my diction-ary or Dickens. Very often we have not exchanged one word.

Mum pushed a bowl of Weet-Bix towards me. Dad had left for work and I had half an hour before the bus for school. Mum was still in her dressing gown and I had the clear impression she'd stay in it for the rest of the day. The bags under her eyes were enormous and heavy. They needed castors and pull-up handles.

'What do you want for your birthday, Pumpkin?' she asked.

'Can I have anything?'

She busied herself with the teapot.

'Within reason. You know we don't have much money.'

'This won't cost anything. I would like Douglas Benson From Another Dimension to come with us to the cemetery tomorrow.'

Mum put the teapot down. She had her back to me, but I could tell her body had tensed. She was as inflexible as wood. Silence stretched.

'No,' she said finally. Just one word, squeezed out, hard and cold.

'Why not?'

She turned towards me and put fingers to the corners of her eyes. Rubbed, like there was a pain there somewhere.

'You know why, Candice,' she said. 'Pumpkin' had been abandoned in favour of 'Candice'. This was not a good sign. 'Family only. We do not invite friends. We do not have a party. We do not celebrate. We pay our respects.'

Most times, I let Mum get away with this. I avoid confrontation because it is always ugly and best avoided. But today, for some reason, I felt the need to argue.

'So why don't we invite Rich Uncle Brian then?' I asked. 'If it is a family-only thing.'

'And you know the answer to that as well, Candice,' she snapped. 'Do not be deliberately stupid.'

'Why can't we celebrate?' I added. I knew this conversation was headed for disaster, but I couldn't stop myself. 'Sky should be celebrated…'

'Her name was Frances.'

'…it should be a cause of joy that she lived, not an excuse for misery because she's dead. I am tired of feeling sad, Mum. I am glad I knew her, but she's gone…'

'Please stop, Candice.'

'…and it's time you accepted that. Sky is dead, Mum, but we aren't…'

'SHUT UP!' I had no time to duck and it probably would have done me no good if I had. The teapot missed my head by a few centimetres and smashed against the wall behind me. It exploded and I felt the prick of porcelain shards against my neck. The shattered handle rolled between my feet, rocked a moment or two and then was still. I raised a hand to my neck and plucked a small sliver from my skin. A thin smear of blood glistened on my index finger.

Mum put a hand to her mouth. Her eyes were wide. We looked at each other for what seemed like minutes, but was probably only a second or two.

'I'm going to school,' I said. I picked up my backpack and headed for the door. Mum remained frozen, but as I left the kitchen she shuddered and rushed after me.

'Candice,' she said at the front door. But I was already halfway down the path.

'Candice, please. I'm sorry, Pumpkin.'

I said nothing. I didn't turn back. Not because I was angry with Mum. Not because I didn't want us to make up. I kept walking because I didn't want her to see the tears in my eyes. And I didn't want to see those that I knew were in hers.

~

'I'm more of a *theoretical* scientist,' said Douglas Benson From Another Dimension.

'Oh,' I said.

'I don't do physical experiments or mess around in labs,' he continued, as if such practices were vaguely unpleasant and undesirable. 'I *think*. All my science is in my head.'

I examined Douglas's head. It was certainly a strange shape. He wore his hair very short and this allowed all the peculiar bumps and depressions of his skull to stand out in relief. Imagine a face drawn on a potato and you'll get the general idea. It was easy to imagine this knobbly orb internally overcrowded with splendid things, jostling for room and position and bulging out due to lack of space. I considered what he said and it struck me that being a *theoretical* something was a perfect state of affairs.

Take Darren Mitford, for example [see 'C Is For Chaos']. He doesn't bother with actually *being* a student in any practical way, like listening, or writing. This saves him time and effort. Maybe he is a *theoretical* student and it is all in his head [I don't think there is much in there, mind you, but a theoretical student wouldn't have to prove it]. I could be a theoretical supermodel or a theoretical postie. The possibilities are exciting.

'Nonetheless,' continued Douglas, 'such a machine would not be difficult to build.' He put one finger to his mouth and rubbed at his lumpy head with the other hand. 'An automatic fish-food dispenser. Hmmmm. A simple timer that releases a valve once a day which in turn dispenses a programmed amount of food directly onto the water's surface. Child's play, really. Why do you want it, Candice?'

'I worry about Earth-Pig Fish's religious temperament,' I replied. 'I am attempting to encourage any atheistic tendencies she might have.'

Douglas Benson From Another Dimension stopped scratching his head and looked at me as if I were mad. In practice, rather than theoretically.

'I see,' he said in a way that showed me he didn't.

'Would you like to come to my birthday party on Sunday?' I said.

'Thank you,' he replied. 'Is it going to be a big party?'

'You, me, Mum and Dad,' I said. 'So twenty-five percent bigger than previous years.'

'I think you'll find that is thirty-three-and-a-third percent bigger,' said Douglas.

'Oh,' I said. 'I'll take your word for it. It's going to be full of drama, though.'

'Why?'

'Because there is a chance I might die a violent death,' I said.

Douglas scratched his head again and squinted at me. I could almost see his thoughts squirming under the surface of his scalp. His head theoretically rippled.

～

Saturday was sunny, so I put on a dress with a bright floral pattern. Rich Uncle Brian had bought it for me a while ago for reasons that were never satisfactorily explained. I looked at myself in my wardrobe mirror. Dirty blonde hair [though I'd just washed it], freckles, flat chest and stick-thin arms and legs. I didn't look like a theoretical supermodel. I looked like a practical one. I found a fascinator tucked at the back of a shelf in the wardrobe and secured it, as best I could, with hairpins. Rich Uncle Brian had once taken me to a horse race and had bought it for me. I hadn't worn it then because it looked like a television aerial stuck to my head and

I was sure it would have scared the horses. It still looked like a television aerial stuck to my head. I finished my outfit with a pair of bright red plastic sunglasses and examined the final effect.

I resembled a scarecrow with a television aerial stuck to its head.

It would do. I went down to the kitchen, prepared for an unpleasant scene. It didn't happen.

Mum and Dad were already there. Dad was getting in pacing practice. He wore his only suit – which was dark and shiny. Mum was dry-eyed, probably because she felt she was an expert in tears and didn't need to rehearse. She wore a black dress. She was as thin as me, but her skin was pale, like sunlight hadn't kissed it in years. It reminded me of cheese left too long in the fridge. Mum looked me up and down and a tendon bunched in her arm. Her mouth opened. Her mouth closed again. Earth-Pig Fish couldn't have done it better. There was silence.

'We'd better go,' she muttered finally.

~

It was a ten-minute drive to the cemetery and no one said a word. Dad parked, unpacked the picnic blanket, a backpack and a bunch of flowers and we trooped through the small gate and along a path winding between headstones. Still no one said a word. Sky's plot was in the middle of the cemetery and I was pleased about that. I liked her at the centre, rather than relegated to the wings. Dad put the backpack on the ground, unfolded the blanket and laid it across the grass at the end of her plot. Mum removed the shrivelled flowers in the vase by the headstone and carefully arranged the new flowers in their place. Then she filled up the vase with water from a bottle she carried in her handbag. Dad started pacing. Mum knelt on the blanket. No one said a word. Again. Mum's shoulders started to shake, though she made no sound. I read the inscription on the headstone, but I kept the words in my head. I always do. I have my routine as well. 'Frances, beloved daughter and sister.' Then the dates when she lived. A short time. Sadder, somehow, for being chiselled in stone.

I stood. Dad paced. Mum knelt.

I wondered what lay beneath the mound of grass. Was there anything left of Sky by now? Worms, and skittering things that like the dark and the damp and the soil, would have been busy. Bones, probably. That's all that would be left. A tiny skeleton, a jumble that could never be put back together. It is difficult to pay respect to bones. Or to words on a headstone. Because Sky could be somewhere – I hoped she *was* somewhere – but I knew the somewhere wasn't here.

I looked up. The sky was fretted with the silhouettes of leaves. Towards a hidden horizon lay a canopy of light, all powdery blue. But over our heads a dark and heavy cloud loomed. I watched the way smoky tendrils curled and shifted in its centre. Suddenly a fat blob of water smacked my forehead and made me flinch. And then another. And another. Dad stopped pacing and hurried to the backpack. He took out three umbrellas, the kind that telescope open at the flick of a switch. He opened one and gave it to Mum. She took it automatically. She held it above her head, but other than that one action, didn't move a muscle. Dad handed me another, took the last one for himself and opened it. He resumed pacing.

I switched my gaze from the cloud above to the tightly furled contraption in my hand. The rain was falling harder now. The silence in the cemetery was replaced by the pitter-patter of falling drops. A lock of hair plastered to my cheek. I liked the rain. It felt as if I was under the world's largest shower. Cold. The leaves on nearby trees shone greener, washed and polished by the rain.

I flicked the switch on my umbrella and it bloomed into a canvas flower, bright with yellow and green stripes. I twirled it so the stripes merged and blurred into each other. Mum knelt in her little cone of dryness.

Dad paced and took his dryness with him. I felt the rain trickle under my collar and run down my back. The umbrella spun before my eyes.

I danced.

I watched a movie once. An old movie. A man was dancing in torrential rain, jumping and splashing in puddles. He used his umbrella, not to keep dry, but for balance. I loved that dance. It made words. It said, *I don't care. I am happy and the rain cannot change that. The world is wonderful. Throw whatever you like at me, I refuse to bend before it. I am happy.*

So I danced. I jumped in puddles. I swung the umbrella in swooping arcs. I smiled and held my head up to the crying sky, welcoming it.

Mum knelt. Dad paced. I danced.

You know the phrase *dysfunctional family*?

Welcome to my world.

IS FOR NEAR-DEATH EXPERIENCE

Douglas Benson From Another Dimension gave me breasts for my birthday.

It was certainly a change from gel pens and I told him that.

'It's certainly a change from gel pens,' I said.

He switched from one foot to another. I had never seen him embarrassed before, but I had read about the signs. Flushing a strange and unnatural shade of red, shifting from foot to foot, unable to make eye contact. Douglas scored three out of three.

'They're very nice,' I said, gazing at the two strange

items on my lap. 'They are the nicest artificial breasts anyone has ever given me.'

That was true, but he spotted the flaw in my statement immediately, probably because he thinks a lot and has strange knobbly lumps on his head.

'I bet they're the *only* artificial breasts you've ever received,' he pointed out.

'That is true,' I replied. 'Certainly.'

He shuffled some more.

'I made them myself,' he muttered.

'Fancy,' I said.

'It's just that…' he went in for more shuffling. I started to worry about bald patches on the carpet. 'You've mentioned…you know…how you were worried about…you know…things not happening… you know…*there*.' He made a general nod to where my chest might be, though, to be honest, the nod was so general and directionless he could have been indicating the cabinet where Mum keeps a collection of glass animals. I couldn't remember mentioning my lack of breasts to Douglas Benson From Another Dimension, but then again, I can't remember *everything* I've ever said. Douglas blurted on, like he had a speech and wanted to get it out before his courage deserted him. 'So I did research on the web about… you know… and what they should be made of. Then it was a simple matter of engineering. They inflate…' He said this with pride as if inflation would win over the most cynical of bosomless doubters. He *almost* made eye contact. '…so you can go from…you know…' He held his own hands against his chest and then moved them out a considerable distance. If I inflated them to that size I'd fall forward and puncture them. I didn't mention this because it would be ungrateful. 'Whatever you want,' he finished.

'They are very nice,' I said. 'I will wear them to the party.'

'Really?' He was so happy he looked at me for a couple of seconds before his eyes slipped away. 'Facsimile Mother said I was mad. She insisted I get you something else.' He handed over another present and I unwrapped it. It was a calligraphy set which was brilliant and an exciting variation on gel pens.

'Thank you, Douglas Benson From Another Dimension,' I said. 'They are lovely presents.'

Douglas had turned up at nine in the morning because I had planned a day out for my birthday. Mum and Dad wanted something simple and straightforward like chicken parmigiana at a local restaurant followed by a birthday cake, a chorus of 'Happy Birthday to you' and an early night. But I insisted. It was my birthday after all.

'You want to wander around a marina in Brisbane, Pumpkin?' said Mum. 'Why?'

'Because Rich Uncle Brian will be there,' I said. 'And he wants to see me on my birthday.'

Mum scratched her head. 'Well, I can understand that, but couldn't you arrange to see him separately? You know he and your dad don't see eye to eye. Couldn't he take you out first and then the three of us could do something later? Go to a restaurant, for example.'

'No,' I said. 'It's my birthday and my choice.' This closed the discussion as it was designed to do.

At nine-thirty we were in the van, heading off to Brisbane. I had my false boobs on under my sweater. I hadn't inflated them and that was a sensible decision. Even so, they made peculiar bumps. My chest looked like Douglas's head. Mum glanced at it [my chest, not Douglas's head] and her mouth opened, then closed again. Then she opened her mouth and closed it again. Another brilliant impersonation of Earth-Pig Fish. In the end, though, she said nothing and simply sat in the front seat. Douglas was next to me in the back. I tried to get everyone singing, but no one was interested. I remembered, in the dim and distant days of family harmony, that we used to sing 'The wheels on the bus go round and round' at the top of our lungs. Dad would do all the motions, putting on the windscreen wipers and tooting the horn at appropriate moments. He didn't care then about the reaction of other motorists. I was tempted to try it, but settled for 'Killing Me Softly [With His Song]' instead. After the first chorus, I got the feeling I was killing them hardly, so I stopped. Mum and Dad stared through the windscreen as if reading the road scrolling beneath the wheels. I talked to Douglas.

'Are you still jumping out of trees?' I asked.

He sighed. 'Of course. But without success, I'm afraid.'

'You fail at jumping out of trees?'

'No. The jumping is no problem. But I can't get back to my world. It is *so* frustrating.'

'Is there a me in your world?'

'What?'

'A Candice Phee? You said there was an infinity of earths and therefore an infinity of me's. So have you bumped into an alternative me in your alternative Earth, and if so, what is she – me – like? Is that alternative Candice your friend? Does she have a religiously-confused fish? Or is she normal?'

I liked the idea of a normal me somewhere, doing normal things and thinking normal thoughts – a Candice who wasn't called a shortened form of Special Needs, who had a boyfriend and a phone, who went to sleepovers and drank cider and liked rap songs and confided everything to her sister, who worshipped her and wanted to be just like her when she grew up.

'You must be there somewhere,' said Douglas, 'but I haven't met you.'

'Will you do me a favour?' I asked. 'If you get back…'

'*When* I get back,' said Douglas.

'Yes. *When* you get back, would you look me up? Say hello from me.' I started to get excited at the possibilities. 'And because you are a whizz at all things scientific, perhaps you could invent something whereby we could communicate between our worlds. Letters, preferably, because I can't do email. And maybe the alternative Candice could be my penpal.' I stopped then, because a horrible thought struck me. What if the alternative Candice was too cool to bother with me? I could cope with the knowledge that Denille was too busy and/or too American to write, but I couldn't face knowing that I didn't like me. So I bit my fingernails, which I do when strange thoughts buzz around my head. If Douglas replied I didn't hear it. I was focused on the probability of being snubbed in an infinite number of worlds.

~

We arrived at the marina in an atmosphere of confusion.

Dad locked the van and we stood for a moment gazing around the car park, which, to be honest, didn't look like the perfect site for birthday celebrations. Neither did the sight of masts bobbing in a strange, detached fashion above the roofs of the cars.

'Well,' said Dad. 'We're here.'

'True,' I said. 'Though, when you think about it, we are always here. I mean, at any given moment, here is inevitably where you must be. You can't be *there*, without moving from the here to the there. And every movement is a small "here". So "here" is a permanent…'

'Candice,' said Dad. 'I know it's your birthday, but please stop. We're here. At the marina, which is your choice. So what do you want to do? Do you want your birthday party in this car park? Nothing would surprise me anymore.'

He started to mutter darkly, so Mum grabbed him by the arm and hauled him off a few metres. There was much waving of arms and subdued growling mingled with the muttering. An occasional word like 'selfish' and 'pig' and 'birthday' fluttered past my ears as well as the odd phrase like 'her day' and 'sarcastic bastard'. These were Mum's contributions. Dad just scowled and muttered. Darkly. *Wonderful*, I thought. I was aiming for harmony, but achieving discord. I took Douglas by the arm and headed towards the boats. Maybe Mum and Dad would notice we'd gone after they'd finished muttering and growling.

'Why *are* we here, Candice?' asked Douglas Benson From Another Dimension.

'To perform a miracle,' I replied.

'Oh,' said Douglas. 'Right.'

I took him straight to the marina. There were so many boats it was difficult to see the water between them, but I knew where I was going. After all, I had thrown up on most of this marina and that helps in the getting of bearings. I saw Rich Uncle Brian's boat at the far end of a long pier and headed towards it.

Now that I was close to the BIG MOMENT, I was becoming nervous. If Rich Uncle Brian and/or Dad didn't respond appropriately I could be moments from an unpleasant death. That got me thinking again, so I stopped.

'Douglas?' I said. 'Do you think there is such a thing as a pleasant death?'

He screwed up his face in concentration. His caterpillar eyebrows writhed.

'Maybe being sucked into a Black Hole,' he replied finally. 'I'm not sure that would be *pleasant*, but it would be amazingly cool. You see, as you approached the event horizon…'

'I thought not,' I said, and took off for the

Motherboard once again. Rich Uncle Brian's yacht bobbed in the water in what sailors would probably find an agreeable fashion. I felt like throwing up. There was no sign of anyone on deck, but Rich Uncle Brian was almost certainly lurking down below, doing whatever nautical people do. I had rung him the day before and he had promised to be there. Rich Uncle Brian keeps his promises. I glanced over my shoulder. Mum and Dad were following, though they were some distance away. I had time to provide important information to Douglas Benson From Another Dimension.

'Douglas,' I said. 'Promise me that whatever happens in the next few minutes, you will do absolutely nothing.'

'What do you mean?' he said.

'I thought it was fairly plain, but I'll rephrase. Promise me that whatever happens in the next few minutes, you will do absolutely nothing.'

'Like what?'

'Like nothing.'

'No.' He shook his head as if to clear away confusion. 'I mean, what will happen?'

'Something.' Suddenly an unpleasant thought surprised me. I was getting plenty of surprising thoughts today. Maybe it had something to do with being a teenager. 'Unless,' I added, 'no one else does anything. If that happens – and ONLY if that happens – I want you to leap around like a mountain goat, screaming, pointing and generally being dramatic. Got it?'

'No,' said Douglas Benson From Another Dimension.

'Good,' I said. 'I'm glad we're on the same wavelength.'

A hundred metres away, Mum and Dad walked along the pier. The time had come. I formed a megaphone with my hands and filled my lungs.

'Rich Uncle Brian!' I yelled. There was a pause while I took in the absence of an uncle on the *Motherboard*'s deck. I geared myself for another bellow, but was spared by the sight of RUB appearing from the bowels of the boat. It was unnerving. A peaked cap rose into view. Underneath it was RUB's head. For a moment it was like a severed head balancing on the boards. Then his shoulders hove into view, followed by the rest of his body. It was like he'd oozed, head first, through the fabric of the boat. I might have applauded, but I had other things on my mind.

'Pumpkin!' he shouted. He might even have waved an arm. I cannot be sure. 'Happy birthday, my girl. Happy birthday!'

'Thank you, Rich Uncle Brian,' I replied.

Then I threw myself off the pier and into the water. It was very wet, which was no great surprise, but also very cold, which was. I resisted the urge to take a sharp intake of breath, which was probably wise.

I sank like a stone and waited. For rescue or death, whichever came first.

I'm confident you'll work out which.

O

IS FOR OBLIVION

This is the way I explained it to Douglas Benson From Another Dimension:

'My family is a mess, Douglas. My father hates my uncle. My uncle loves my father, but cannot back down. My mother is torn by family loyalties. I thought if my uncle and my father were united in a common purpose [saving me from drowning], they would forget their differences and bond. I pictured them throwing themselves into the water, hauling me to the surface. One clearing my airways while the other performed mouth-to-mouth resuscitation. And then, while I spluttered and drew breath, there would be much weeping and wailing. But there would also be hugging and tears of joy. A reconciliation.'

'You're an idiot, Candice,' replied Douglas.

'Yes,' I said. 'Certainly.'

It hadn't happened like that.

Rich Uncle Brian *had* thrown himself overboard [so Douglas Benson From Another Dimension reported to me later], but hit his head on the side of the neighbouring yacht. Luckily he did no damage to it. The yacht, I mean. His head was another matter. Dad hurled himself off the pier while trying to take off his jacket in the time-honoured Hollywood fashion. Being a computer geek, however, he couldn't get his arms out. As a result he fluttered like a wounded bird and cracked his head against Rich Uncle Brian's knee. The two floated in a growing pool of blood-stained water and had to be rescued by the captain of a neighbouring yacht.

My mother fainted.

Douglas Benson From Another Dimension was confused about my instructions. I'd told him to act ONLY if nobody did anything. Someone [in fact, everyone] *had* done something, so he stood for a minute or two working through the problem. His logical mind told him to stand still, but I *had* been underwater for some time and showed no signs of resurfacing. Eventually he leaped around like a mountain goat, screaming, pointing and generally being dramatic. Unfortunately there was no one still conscious who could pay attention so he jumped into the ocean as well.

Frankly, by this time, he might as well, since anyone who was anyone was either floating or thrashing about madly. With the exception of my mother, that is.

And me, of course.

While all the excitement was happening on the surface, I was sinking deeper into cold and darkness. Part of me wondered why the rescue was taking so long. But mostly I watched the images floating before my eyes.

They say that when you're dying your whole life flashes before your eyes. It's a slight exaggeration. I saw my mother when she was younger, before she had forgotten how to smile. I saw Dad and Rich Uncle Brian laughing and joking together. I saw Douglas Benson From Another Dimension jumping from a tree and fading from sight before he hit the ground. I saw Earth-Pig Fish floating on the surface of her bowl. I saw Sky. Not as a baby, but as she would be now. She was saying something, but I couldn't work out what it was. Her face was serious, though, and I could tell by her eyes that what she wanted to say was very important. It was a curious mixture of images from my life and [maybe] images from beyond my death.

I didn't know what to make of it.

It was Sky's face that saved me. That and Douglas Benson From Another Dimension's birthday present. I cannot remember doing this, but I must have pressed the trigger of the can that I'd put in my pocket before we set off. The can that was connected by a plastic tube to my false breasts. It was the passion in Sky's face that pressed that trigger. I don't want to get mystical, but my dead sister was yelling at me to *do* something. She was pulling me from death, from joining her. I read it in her face.

The can injected pressurised air into my false breasts, which inflated to maximum size. In effect I was now wearing 10DDD floaties and they catapulted me to the surface, where I must have made a dramatic entrance, like a strangely endowed dolphin jumping through a hoop. Luckily, no one threw me a fish. Douglas Benson From Another Dimension dragged me to the pier where people, alerted by the drama, pulled me onto dry land. Well, dry wood, since I was lying next to my unconscious mother. Her eyelids fluttered open and her gaze went to my chest. One breast had deflated in the trauma of my impersonation of a surface-to-air missile. The other ballooned in a bizarre fashion.

I vomited.

My mother fainted again.

Douglas Benson From Another Dimension kissed me.

It was my first kiss and it was strange. His lips were cold and wet and I had vomited a bucketful of salty water, so it wasn't in ideal conditions. But I remember wondering why people made such a fuss of it.

For all that, I was glad he did it.

The rest of my birthday passed in a haze. Two ambulances arrived. One took Dad and Rich Uncle Brian to hospital, while the other took me, Mum and Douglas Benson From Another Dimension. This was not the most harmonious of combinations. I would have mentioned this, but the paramedics were too busy applying an oxygen mask to my face to listen. I heard later that Dad woke up on the journey and found himself centimetres away from his brother. In his concussed state, Dad remembered that Rich Uncle Brian had kneed him in the head, preventing him from rescuing his daughter. So he tried to strangle RUB and had to be restrained.

How would I rate the success of my plan to reconcile my family? On a scale of zero to ten?

Around minus-fifteen.

Still, I didn't have to eat chicken parmigiana and listen to a chorus of 'Happy Birthday To You'. That was a silver lining. The majority of the cloud, however, was still very dark.

IS FOR PICOULT

'I would like to see Mr Dawson, please.'

'Do you have an appointment?'

This was always going to be tricky. Effective oral communication was vital, so I had written a variety of notes in advance to cover all eventualities. As you know, I am not comfortable with the spoken word when dealing with people for the first time. I sorted through the sheaves of paper in my hand and passed her a sheet.

No. But tell him Candice Phee is here.

He will want to see me.

This always works in movies.

I have no idea why.

The receptionist glanced at the note and gave a look that said she thought I was at least one sandwich short of a picnic. Possibly an entire hamper. I am used to this, so I ignored her. She looked me up and down and didn't appear impressed. Then she picked up her phone.

'Mr Dawson? There is a young lady here who would like to see you. Her name is Candice Phee and she doesn't have an appointment.' I detected mockery in her pronunciation of the word 'lady', but she had a picture on her desk of a small child smiling so I forgave her. She was obviously a loving and caring mother. If not necessarily a loving and caring receptionist.

She listened for a moment and then turned to me.

'What is it about?'

I shuffled through my sheaf of papers and found the right one.

It is a delicate matter which will test his litigious powers. I cannot be more specific at this stage, but it will be a case that will attract national and possibly international media interest. It will seal Mr Dawson's reputation as a formidable lawyer. When he hears the nature of the case, he will, I am sure, offer his services pro bono. *If he scratches my back, I will scratch his. I speak metaphorically. Unless he really does have an itch, in which case I can be flexible.*

I was pleased with the pro bono bit. It is Latin and means 'for free'. Mr Dawson would clearly respect a client with a firm grip of legal terminology. The receptionist read the letter, curled her lip and spoke into the phone.

'She doesn't know, but she wants it for free.'

This was not fair, but I decided to hold my peace. Anyway, I didn't have a note to cover this eventuality.

'He will see you. Second door on your right.'

I gathered up my pile of papers and followed the instructions. I knocked on the door, waited for a mumbled 'come in' and entered Mr Dawson's office. He sat behind a large desk cluttered with briefs – by this, I mean papers about court cases rather than underwear. He glanced up as I came in. Mr Dawson was bald and his face looked like it had been slept in. Heavy jowls and a mournful expression. A picture came to mind of a bulldog on tranquillisers. This was exciting. I could imagine him in a white, powdered wig, addressing a jury, objecting to opposing counsel and resting his case. I felt certain I had chosen the right person.

'What can I do for you?' he said.

I handed him a note and he peered at it over small rimless spectacles. This was a good touch and he rose further in my estimation. He handed the note back.

'I'm sorry, I don't understand,' he said.

I read the note myself.

Sorry I haven't completed the assignment yet,
Miss Bamford, but the matter is well in hand.

No wonder he didn't understand. I'd given him the wrong note. Why had I brought that one along anyway? I flicked through my sheaf, found the correct one and passed it over. He read again, glanced up at me once and then re-read the note. I waited patiently and resisted the strong urge to hum. Finally, he put the note on his desk and peered at me over the top of his specs. His expression was difficult to read.

'You want me to take legal action against your parents so you are removed from their house and placed under local authority care? In effect, you want to divorce them and find foster parents?'

'Correct,' I replied. I trusted myself with that word and hadn't felt the need to write it down. 'Certainly,' I added, which was testament to my confidence.

Mr Dawson gazed at me for a moment, took off his glasses and rubbed at the corners of his eyes.

'You haven't been reading Jodi Picoult, have you?' he asked. His voice seemed tired. '*My Sister's Keeper*?'

Actually, I hadn't read the novel. I'd seen the movie and cried for two hours. It's about a girl who brings a legal case against her parents, who use her as an organ donor for her elder sister, who suffers from a life-threatening disease. The girl hires a lawyer who takes the case to court in a bid to win the right to refuse to continue organ donation. It was the movie that had given me my brilliant idea. I didn't really want to divorce my parents, but I hoped the shock of receiving a court summons would bring them to their senses. There would be wailing, of course. But there would also be hugs and promises and family holidays and choruses of 'The wheels on the bus go round and round.' All of this, however, was too complicated to explain and I hadn't brought notes covering this area, so I played safe.

'Correct,' I said again.

Mr Dawson sighed.

'You do know what kind of a legal expert I am, don't you?' he said. I shook my head. 'Property conveyancing,' he continued. 'I deal with contracts related to house purchasing, rental properties, business premises. I do not go in front of judges. I do not address juries. I never shout "I object" or "I rest my case." I do not have a powdered wig. I don't even have an unpowdered wig.'

I thought about this.

'Sounds dull,' I said.

'It is,' said Mr Dawson. 'It is very, very dull. But it is what I do.'

'I could probably provide the wig,' I said. I remembered there was one hanging up in the window at the party-hire shop where I had bought Miss Bamford's eye patch.

IS FOR QUESTIONS

Dear Denille,

I have questions and queries buzzing in my head. Queries and questions, questions and queries. Round and round they go.

I'm sorry to burden you with them, but, frankly, I don't have anyone else to turn to. Under different circumstances I would talk to Earth-Pig Fish, but, as I have explained before, I worry she will interpret my attempts at communication as divine intervention, thus increasing her religious confusion. All I can do is hurl her fish food into the bowl from a *considerable distance and beat a hasty retreat.*

This is not ideal for her (it makes big splashes) and not ideal for me (I miss her advice – and sometimes the bowl).

Question 1: *Why are lawyers in New York very young, intelligent, exceptionally well-dressed and bursting with enthusiasm?*

Is it just that they are American? I ask because I visited a lawyer yesterday in an effort to divorce my parents. I made little progress, in part because the lawyer in question was more interested in Property Conveyancing (whatever that might be). Based upon my television viewing (such as it is), it seems you can't throw a stone in New York without hitting a lawyer prepared to take on a juicy case like the one I presented. My lawyer might have been intelligent, but he was missing the other characteristics (youth, a stylish suit, enthusiasm and United States citizenship). This is not surprising. If he was all of those things he would certainly be in New York, which never sleeps, rather than in Albright, which does little else.

He showed me the door, Denille.

I don't mean he pointed out all the interesting characteristics of the door (if there

were any), but rather that he asked me to
leave. I did, after giving him my home phone
number should he change his mind. His body
language did not leave me feeling optimistic.

Follow-up Question 2: *Why do American televi-
sion lawyers look like surgically enhanced Year 11*
students?*

Over here, it takes years and years to
become a lawyer. Over there, most seem to get
a licence to practice when they hit puberty.

It is possible I am mistaken, so please
correct me if that is so. Anyway, none of this is
relevant. So, better yet, don't correct, ignore.

I wanted to divorce my parents because
they failed to rally round after I escaped a
watery death only through a birthday gift
of inflatable breasts. I trust I make myself
clear. I felt the threat of divorce would focus
their minds. This is no longer an option.

Question 3: *If kisses are so wonderful, why are*
they sloppy and messy, and why do they involve*
exchanging bodily fluids?*

I believe you will be a fount of information
on this subject because, being American and

called Denille, I assume you spend much time at high school lip-locked with football players (and possibly baseball players).

To place this question in context, I should explain that Douglas Benson From Another Dimension kissed me after I escaped death. This was the first time I had been kissed, but, as it turned out, not the last. Yesterday, I went to his ravine, as always, in case he tried to transport across dimensions by throwing himself off the edge. He turned up, which gave me quite a start. In my worst nightmares I see him blurring across my vision and plummeting to oblivion. Instead, he sat next to me.

'What are you doing here, Candice?' he said. This was, under the circumstances, a reasonable question.

'I'm here to stop you killing yourself,' I replied.

I am addicted to the truth, Denille, which occasionally causes problems. I explained my reasoning.

'You mustn't worry,' he said. 'I won't jump off the ravine. I promise.'

I was relieved, but needed further information. 'Why?'

'Because if I can't get back to my own dimension,' he replied, 'there will be some compensation.'

My last question had been an overwhelming success, so I tried again.

'Why?'

'Because I love you,' he said. Then he kissed me. For the second time.

Now I know that you are meant to close your eyes when a boy kisses you (or a girl, I imagine. I don't see why it should be gender-specific), but I was fascinated by the close-up of his face, which the situation afforded. I saw his pores, a couple of which were clogged and on the fast track to zits. This wasn't romantic, as I understand the word. Apparently, the pressure of lips is also meant to be pleasurable. Tingles are supposed to run down your spine. My spine was tingle-free. I checked. His tongue then pushed through my lips. It was large and the texture of certain meats that my mother used to try to get me to eat when I was younger. I resisted it then and I resisted it with Douglas. I am not altogether comfortable with my own spit. Swallowing someone else's did not fill me with desire.

And love? Everything I have read suggests the emotion of love is so intense it cannot be mistaken. Stomachs plummet. Blood races. Heartbeats quicken. My stomach stayed stationary. My blood plodded. My heartbeat slowed because it was keeping pace with my blood. Obviously I cannot comment on what was happening to Douglas Benson From Another Dimension's body.

The point I am making is that kissing is supposed to be nice. This wasn't. It was messy. And that leads me to:

Question 4: *Am I weird?*

One positive from all this was that when Douglas Benson From Another Dimension had finished trying to find my tonsils with his tongue, he leaned back and a worried expression swept his face.

'The thing is, Candice,' he said, 'I must get back to my own world. I simply have no option.' He ran his hands over the knobbly contours of his head. Then he lowered his voice. 'Even if it breaks your heart.'

'Oh, okay,' I said.

'But I will find you – the alternative you – in my world. Is it too much to expect that we could be soulmates across different dimensions?'

'Probably,' I replied, but I don't think he heard me.

'Then again, we might be destined to remain star-crossed lovers.'

'Righty ho.'

Anyway, as you can imagine, all this was exciting in a distasteful way and I felt I had made a dramatic start to my teens (I have just turned thirteen — don't worry about sending a card). I supposed this made Douglas Benson From Another Dimension my boyfriend, rather than just my friend who is a boy. There is a big difference, it seems, though I cannot explain it.

But then everything became really exciting.

'I have a solution for the goldfish problem,' he said. This struck me as an abrupt change of subject, but that was fine by me. I wasn't getting along very well with the old one.

'You've made an automatic feeder for Earth-Pig Fish?' I guessed.

'No. Much better. A simple solution. I'll come to your house tomorrow and show you.'

Exceptionally exciting. If Douglas Benson From Another Dimension can pull this off, I'd be prepared to let him kiss me again. I just wouldn't like it.

Best wishes,
Your penpal,
Candice

. . . .

IS FOR RELIEF TEACHERS

. . . .

Douglas Benson From Another Dimension insisted on holding my hand when we entered Miss Bamford's classroom the following morning. It was better than getting up close and personal with his tongue, though his hand *was* slightly clammy. Why is romance so wet?

Jen Marshall choked on her chewing gum.

'Hey,' she yelled. 'Get a load of this, guys.' She shrieked with laughter. 'The retards have got together. Oh. My. God.' She fell onto the floor and rolled around, clutching her belly. There is always something dramatic about Jen. You have to admire her.

'Ignore her, Candice,' said Douglas Benson From Another Dimension. 'She's jealous.'

That stopped Jen Marshall's rolling.

'Jealous?' she screamed. 'Jealous? Of what, you… you…' [She's good on drama. Not so good on vocabulary.] 'Retard!' she finished.

I might have pointed out her unnecessary repetition, but I was worried about that chewing gum.

'Jen?' I said. 'If you are going to shout, it might be an idea to dispose of your gum. Accidents have been known to happen, you know…'

'Shut up, moron,' she yelled. [If I have a criticism of Jen, it's that she doesn't vary her vocal volume.] 'Shut the hell up.'

'What is going on here?'

The bellow made Jen's screams seem like a delicate whisper. Twenty-five heads snapped around to the front of the classroom. Forty-nine ears rang [Alex McLean, missing one ear drum]. We froze in various poses. We were expecting Miss Bamford. We didn't get her.

The woman at the front of the class was tall and stick-insect-thin, as if she'd been left to dry in the sun for a long time. Her eyes swept the room and might have turned us all to statues, if we weren't already turned to statues. Now, I have met many forbidding people, teachers in particular, and I have never failed to spot some sign of kindness in them. The glint of an eye. The relaxed cast of an arm. The hint of a smile. This woman gave no sign of friendliness. I felt that in a battle between her and a saltwater crocodile, the smart money would be on her.

I liked her. Immediately.

'Sit down! This instant!'

We sat. Even Jen Marshall hurried to get to her chair, and Jen Marshall hurries for nothing and no one. The stick-insect [crossed with a saltwater crocodile] waited for a moment and then sat at the teacher's desk. She treated us to another sweep of steely intent, which we received in silence. She placed her hands, palms down, on the desk.

'My name is Miss Cowie and I am a relief teacher. This does not mean I have an invisible target between my eyes or that you should confuse me with a human being.'

Judging by the expressions on my classmates' faces, there was little chance of that.

'Miss Bamford is unfortunately ill and will be away for a few days. In the meantime, I am in charge. She has left instructions that you are to prepare for the end-of-term exam. I will hand out a practice paper, involving close reading. You have this lesson to finish it. You will work in silence.'

The examination was fairly easy. I opened my pencil case, selected my favourite pens and started to work. Even Jen Marshall worked in silence. Miss Cowie sat at the front of the class, but she didn't read or open a laptop. This was unusual. In my experience, relief teachers generally read the newspaper or knitted or surfed the internet or [in one memorable instance] built a small fighter jet from tiny plastic parts. Miss Cowie sat as if she had a steel rod inserted in her spine. She watched us. She did not flinch. Her eyes never rested.

I worried about Miss Bamford, though. After all, she is my favourite teacher in the whole world.

When I got home, things were different. Mum was up and bustling around the kitchen. Dad was slicing onions. No computer parts hung from his extremities, which was a surprise. I checked twice. He was, however, sporting a large bruise on his left cheekbone where Rich Uncle Brian's knee had presumably made contact.

'Hello,' I said. The greeting wasn't exciting, but it rarely failed.

'Hello, Pumpkin,' said Mum. She gave me a huge smile. Dad put his knife down and tousled my hair. I was glad he'd remembered to put down the knife. 'Hi, Candice,' he said. 'How was school?'

My head was buzzing with questions, but it was polite to answer questions already asked before posing your own.

'Wonderful,' I said. 'We had a relief teacher today. It is not clear if she is human. She confessed to being unsure herself. She ruled the class with an iron fist and steely eyes and possibly other metallic body parts. Jen Marshall wrote something. No one knew she could. I believe she shocked herself.'

'Lovely,' said Mum, which struck me as a strange response.

'What's happening?' I asked.

'I'm making dinner,' said Mum. Her bright smile was unnerving.

'And I'm helping,' added Dad.

'What's happening?' I said.

'I thought we'd have a family dinner and a nice chat,' said Mum. She spread her arms in a gesture of appeal. 'Is that so unusual?'

'Yes,' I said.

I felt no one could argue with that statement, and no one did. Dad took up the knife again and continued dicing onions. Mum scrutinised a recipe book. Had I wandered into the wrong family by mistake? I thought about checking the number on the front door, but decided against it.

'Douglas Benson From Another Dimension is coming round in a few minutes,' I said. 'He has a solution to the Earth-Pig Fish problem. Can he stay for dinner?'

Mum glanced at Dad. Dad glanced at Mum. Both of them glanced at me. I'd never experienced so much glancing in the Phee household. Then they glanced at each other again. Dad broke the sequence.

'Sorry, Candice,' he said. 'Nothing against Douglas, you understand, but we need to have…a private chat. In fact, your mum suggested I take you to the park while she finishes dinner. Maybe Douglas could eat with us some other time.'

'A chat?' I said.

'Yes,' said Mum. 'It's long overdue.'

'Like a library book?' I asked.

Mum and Dad did the glancing thing again, but I never found out what they might have said because there was a knock on the front door. I was the obvious choice to answer it, so I did.

'Hello, Douglas Benson From Another Dimension,' I said.

'Hi, Candice.' He had his hands behind his back and a broad smile on his face. I was anxious to know what was behind that smile and that back. 'No peeking,' he added. 'Close your eyes.'

I did because I like darkness. Some people are afraid of the dark. If anything, I am afraid of the light. Douglas took me by the hand and led me down the hallway to my bedroom. I assumed it was my bedroom, but I couldn't see because my eyes were closed. He sat me down on my bed [I assumed] and there was general rustling, punctuated by an abrupt splash.

'Open your eyes, now, Candice,' he said. I did. His smile was still there but his hands were empty. In the goldfish bowl there were two fish. One was Earth-Pig Fish, obviously. The other was an intruder. They swam round each other – one clockwise, the other anti-clockwise. The chances of crashing appeared high.

I tore my eyes away and turned to Douglas Benson From Another Dimension.

'Why?' I asked.

Douglas sat next to me on the bed. He was excited.

'It's logical, Candice,' he said. 'You worried your fish might think of you as God. That was why you wanted an automatic feeding system. But I got to thinking. If you had one of those, the fish might find that was even more mysterious. Food would appear like magic. And I hypothesised that such a miracle might make things worse. Maybe the fish would worship the feeding machine and that would be more alarming than worshipping you. It would be a false idol.'

Douglas is *so* smart. He had obviously earned every one of those knobbly bits on his head. I wanted to tell him that, but didn't want to interrupt his flow.

'The solution was obvious. Another fish. This way they keep each other company, they will each find things in the other to fascinate. This should prevent religious thoughts. They might even fall in love.' He turned his eyes to my doona. 'Like you and me,' he added.

Was Earth-Pig Fish ready for romance? I had no way of knowing, but I liked the way Douglas Benson From Another Dimension was thinking. I stood and approached the bowl. The new fish was smaller than Earth-Pig Fish and had a tiny black blotch on his head. Was it my imagination or was Earth-Pig Fish moving with more purpose? Was this the dawning of love? It occurred to me that if she kissed the new fish at least she would be well prepared for the wetness, on account of the fact that this was her normal medium.

'What will you call him?' asked Douglas.

'That's easy,' I said. 'His name will be Skullcap-Fish.'

'Because of that black spot?'

'In part,' I replied. 'But mainly because one of the last proper words in the dictionary is "zucchetto", a small cap worn by members of the clergy. Aardvark and zucchetto. They are alpha and omega. They complete a circle.'

Douglas bent his head close to mine and we watched the fish pirouette around each other. For a moment I thought he was going to broach the subject of kissing, but he didn't.

'Thank you, Douglas,' I said. 'You are the most brilliant person from another dimension I have ever known. But I've thought of a problem.'

'Yes?'

'What if Earth-Pig Fish thinks Skullcap-Fish has been created especially for her? What if she thinks they are Eve and Adam and the bowl is a Garden of Eden? That plastic frond on the bottom could be their tree of knowledge.'

'Oh shut up, Candice,' said Douglas Benson From Another Dimension. 'You think too much.'

And he kissed me for the third time.

It was just as messy as the previous two, but it gave me time to think. Douglas was right. It was likely that Earth-Pig and Skullcap would develop a relationship, have arguments, refuse to talk to each other and become miserable. They would be a normal family.

❧

Dad and I walked to the park. It was a beautiful day and the sky was dusted with delicate wisps of cloud. I carried his remote-controlled plane. It was surprisingly light and the wingspan was broad. Up there in the sky it didn't appear so big, but that was all about perspective, I supposed. I didn't want to think about perspective. I wanted to know what Dad was going to say. My family had never really gone in for chats, and part of me welcomed the opportunity.

The main part of me worried.

When we got to the park, Dad started the plane's engine. In moments it was sweeping and swooping through the sky. It looked like a bird. I sat on the grass and watched Dad. His shoulders were relaxed, his eyes fixed on the plane.

'We had a phone call earlier,' he said. 'From a Mr Dawson.'

'Ah,' I said.

S

IS FOR SCHISMS

'That's nice,' I added after a considerable pause.

'Not really,' said Dad. 'He said you wanted to divorce us. Apparently, the only thing that stopped him taking the case was because he is a house conveyancer.'

'Ah,' I said again. I felt this wasn't very forthcoming under the circumstances, so I added: 'Hmmm. House conveyancing.'

'Do you want to tell me what that was all about?'

'No thanks,' I said. 'But I think you should know that Douglas Benson From Another Dimension has solved the Earth-Pig Fish problem.'

'Do you really want to divorce us?' It was irritating

that Dad wouldn't look at me. His head was tilted towards the plane. It buzzed and whined. It banked behind a tree and for a moment was lost to view. Then it reappeared and Dad's fingers danced over the controls.

'Yes,' I said. 'No,' I added. Then, just to make sure I had covered all the bases, 'I don't know.' Actually, all of those replies were true.

'I don't understand.'

'Douglas bought me another fish,' I said. 'To keep Earth-Pig Fish company. But there is a possibility that we might be creating a Garden of Eden scenario, which would put me back to square one as far as religion is concerned.'

'I'm not talking about your fish, Candice. As you well know.'

'Oh,' I said. 'Are you sure you don't want to?' I added. 'It's a fascinating subject.'

'What are you doing?'

'Dad?' I said. 'Why do you have to watch your plane all the time?'

He sighed.

'I would have thought that was obvious, Candice. If I don't, I will lose control and it will crash.'

'Isn't that the same with families?' I asked.

He looked at me when I said that. The plane made

a strange whining noise. Out of the corner of my eye I saw it catch a branch of a tree. There was a distant crump and small pieces of plastic and leaves floated, gently, delicately, to the ground.

~

The meal was ready when Dad and I got back from the park. Dad carried what was left of his plane and I took the remote control. I felt sorry for him, especially since it had been my question that had caused the crash, but I didn't quite know how to express it. Dad said nothing either.

I put out knives and forks while Mum and Dad had a muttered conversation. Judging by the way they kept glancing at me, it wasn't tricky to work out the topic. I hummed. I knew the inquisition wasn't over yet. It would accompany the spaghetti bolognaise. Under different circumstances, I would have welcomed this side dish. In this circumstance, I would have preferred garlic bread.

Mum pushed spaghetti around her plate. It made interesting patterns.

I watched the parmesan melt into my sauce. It made interesting patterns too.

'Pumpkin?' she said. 'Your accident on the marina. Falling into the water. Was that really an accident?'

I considered introducing the subject of Earth-Pig

Fish and Skullcap-Fish into the dinner conversation at that point. Possibly, Mum would be so intrigued by all the religious implications she'd forget the original topic. She might even get so carried away she'd actually put some of the spaghetti into her mouth rather than using it as an artistic medium. It was a million-to-one shot, though, so I reverted to my default position. Honesty.

'No,' I said. The following silence was so heavy you could weigh and bag it.

Dad put down his fork. 'You tried to kill yourself?' he said.

'No,' I said.

'I don't understand,' Mum said.

'Neither do I,' Dad said.

'That makes it unanimous,' I said.

I thought for a moment Mum was going to get *very* angry. She put a hand to her forehead as if to check on a pain. Then she rubbed her eyes. Her face was red. She took a sip from her wine glass and her hand shook. She was obviously struggling to keep control. I pushed my spaghetti bolognaise around the plate on the principle that if you can't beat them you should join them. I waited.

'Okay, Candice,' she said finally. 'I want total honesty. In return I promise we will not get angry. But...' she shook her head. 'I need to know – *we* need to know – what is wrong. Why you have done these things. So let's start at the marina. Why did you…do what you did?'

'I was trying to save our family,' I said.

I explained how I had seen it unfold in my head. Dad and Rich Uncle Brian united in rescuing me. A family bonded.

Mum bent over her food while I talked and I saw a tear fall onto her plate. Instantly I felt…not remorse. I had to tell the truth. I felt sad. It oozed from me, like sweat.

'You think our family needs saving?' Dad said.

'Yes.' I said. I thought about Mum in her bedroom and Dad in his shed. We were drowning. But no one was throwing themselves in the water after us. So we splashed in our own separate circles. It was only a matter of time before we became exhausted and sank. I decided not to share this.

'And how would divorcing us help?' said Dad. 'Would you really prefer living with strangers?'

'You *are* strangers,' I said and Mum sobbed, a short gasp quickly choked. 'Anyway,' I continued, 'Rich Uncle Brian would take me in.' Dad flinched, so I hurried on. 'But I don't want to live with him. I just want you back. That's why I've done what I've done. I'm sorry.'

I meant sorry for the upset, not sorry for my actions. But I was tired from all the talking and didn't want to explain any further.

Mum wiped her face on her napkin and made as if to leave the table. Then, with an effort of will, she forced herself to stay. She picked up her fork, pushed around some more spaghetti and then gave up. She straightened her back and looked me full in the eyes.

'You are right!' she said. Her voice was loud and shrill. She laughed, but it sounded all wrong. 'You are absolutely right. We are appalling parents. We should never have had children. It's a small miracle we only lost the one. It's more than we deserve.'

Then she kicked back her chair, which fell on its side and rocked for a moment. Mum's face twisted and a strange, keening noise came from her throat. She turned and rushed from the room. The bedroom door was slammed shut.

Dad and I sat for a moment, but we didn't even have the energy to push spaghetti around.

~

I have a computer chair in my bedroom. I do not have a computer. Rich Uncle Brian bought it for me [the chair, not the non-existent computer]. I explained to RUB that Earth-Pig Fish's bowl was like a computer because I could stare at the glass and get information without the threat of viruses. What's more I didn't have to boot it up. I don't know why computers have to be booted up. It seems exceptionally violent to me, but I am not good, as must be clear by now, at technical matters.

I hadn't used the computer chair for a long time because of The God Problem, but now I sat and wheeled myself in front of the bowl. I bent my face towards the plastic world and watched my fish as they circumnavigated it. I paid particular attention to their reaction when my face ballooned into their vision. It's difficult to be certain, but I didn't notice any obvious change in their movements. There wasn't a pause, as I felt sure there must be on beholding the miraculous. I was encouraged. So I started talking to my fish. I talked to both of them and hoped Earth-Pig Fish wouldn't be resentful that I was including Skullcap-Fish, who [to be fair] hadn't been around long enough to earn my confidence.

Dad knocked on my door ten minutes later. I was tired of all the talking, but couldn't think of how I could turn him away. He sat on the edge of my bed and rested his hands on his knees. We sat in silence for a moment or two.

'How's Mum?' I asked.

He sighed.

'Better, Candice,' he said. 'I think she's sleeping now.'

'Is she bipolar?'

I had looked this up in one of the encyclopaedias at school. It has nothing to do with the North Pole and the South Pole, even though, when you think about it, the world *is* bi-polar. [Does that mean there are bipolar bears up in the Arctic?] It's a condition involving fluctuations between moods of deep despair and moods that are…well, normal. It seemed to fit Mum.

'No one has put a name to it,' said Dad. 'She's depressed, Candice. Deeply depressed. She has her good days and her bad days.'

'Can it be cured?'

Dad rubbed at his eyes. He appeared desperately tired.

'Depression is complicated. There is no simple cure,' he said. 'Though some drugs can help. Trouble is, your mum doesn't like the medication. She doesn't want chemicals messing with her brain, and I can't say I blame her. But who knows? Maybe it's time to give them a go again. Perhaps I can persuade her.'

'Are you depressed, Dad?' I asked.

'Me? No. I'm just…a failure, I guess.'

'Why?'

'It's complicated, Candice. I work hard at my job, but it doesn't satisfy me. It barely covers the bills either. What I should be doing is writing programs. It's what I was put on this earth to do. I try in my spare time.

But I can't seem to make a go of that either. Whatever I touch fails.'

'Unlike Rich Uncle Brian,' I said.

Dad flinched.

'Unlike Rich Uncle Brian,' he said. I was expecting dark muttering, but I didn't get it. He slapped his hands onto his knees. 'Perhaps it's time I gave up, Candice. Accept the inevitable. It's all very well to have dreams, but not when they threaten to destroy your own family. You deserve better.'

'I don't want you to give up your dreams, Dad,' I said.

'And I don't want them to rule my life,' he replied. 'That's when they turn into nightmares. And we've all had a skinful of nightmares.'

'I'm not giving up on my dreams and you shouldn't either,' I said.

Dad laughed and tousled my hair.

'Good on you, Candice,' he said. He got to his feet. 'I'd better do the dishes,' he added. 'They won't do themselves.'

'Do you need help?'

'Would you like to help?'

'No,' I said.

Dad laughed. 'Then don't worry.' He closed my bedroom door, but immediately opened it again.

'You know what we all need, Candice?' he asked.

'Love?' I suggested. 'And a new remote-controlled plane?'

'A holiday,' said Dad. 'It would do us the world of good.' He closed the door again.

Earth-Pig Fish and Skullcap-Fish listened while I told them my brilliant idea, but they made no response. Perhaps they were becoming wrapped up in each other. That was okay. Neither of them paid attention to the plastic frond at the bottom of the bowl, so if it *was* a Tree of Knowledge, it wasn't tempting them. That was good. I wanted them to remain innocent.

I wanted all of us to remain innocent.

~

Later, I tiptoed down the corridor and rang Rich Uncle Brian. The house was silent. Dad must have gone to bed or maybe he'd retired to his shed again to pursue a dream or two.

'Hello, Rich Uncle Brian,' I said when he picked up. 'I wondered if you would like to buy me a hamburger of dubious origin?'

'Now?'

'No. Tomorrow.'

'Of course, Pumpkin,' he said. 'I'll pick you up from school.'

'Wonderful, Rich Uncle Brian,' I said. 'It is not food

that motivates me, though I won't turn down dim sims, but I want to discuss finance. As you are a rich uncle, I felt you were qualified.'

There was that puzzled pause at the end of the line again, but, as I've said before, this is customary between me and Rich Uncle Brian, so I ignored it.

'Should there be time,' I added. 'I will tell you about the dramatic turn of events involving Earth-Pig Fish. It is a story worthy of Charles Dickens himself, though it's unlikely he will write it since he's dead.'

The silence extended, so I cut it off. 'See you tomorrow, Rich Uncle Brian,' I said and hung up.

Then I went to bed with my dictionary. I'd finished Z, but I was anxious to start again. In my experience it's almost impossible to tire of aardvarks.

T

IS FOR TALKING

Miss Cowie handed back our assignments the following day. I got an A−, which worried me. I always get straight A's with Miss Bamford [apart from the Alphabet Assignment, which, for obvious reasons, I hadn't handed in yet]. Was Miss Bamford too generous or Miss Cowie too harsh? Life is complicated. I toyed with the idea of writing Miss C a note asking for her views on this, but decided against it. My notes are, apparently, an acquired taste. And I couldn't talk to the relief teacher. By my reckoning, we were a few weeks away from that. By which time Miss B would be back. I hoped.

At the end of the lesson, Miss Cowie dropped a

bombshell. I don't mean she exploded a dangerous device in the classroom. No teacher, to my knowledge, has done that. I speak metaphorically.

'Tomorrow,' she said, 'we will start work on the next component of the course. You have finished autobiography…' [*Oops*, I thought.] '…and now we will move on to biography. As you know, a biography is a record of someone else's life. I have decided we will start small. I will pair you up and you'll spend tomorrow's lesson interviewing each other, making notes for an oral presentation on the important aspects of your partner's life.'

Silence greeted this pronouncement. Once again, I was worried. At least half the class were people I had never spoken to. It was going to be extremely difficult interviewing someone purely by writing questions on a sheet of notepaper. Plus it would probably anger Miss Cowie, though I hoped Miss Bamford might have told her about me. As it turned out, I needn't have worried.

'Candice Phee, you will be paired with Jennifer Marshall.'

I smiled. I like Jen. I turned in my chair to share my smile.

Jen looked like she'd swallowed a wasp. She opened her mouth [to protest, I imagine], but probably because she also chose that moment to take a sharp intake of breath, her chewing gum lodged in the back of her throat, causing her complexion to change to an interesting shade of blue. She recovered quickly, but by that time the bell had rung and her chance to protest had gone.

I was looking forward to tomorrow. I thought Jen Marshall must have led an interesting life. I also felt our conversation would undoubtedly cement our friendship, making it solid and stable. Like cement.

~

Rich Uncle Brian slid into the bench opposite me and smiled. I couldn't help glancing at the purplish bruise on his temple, just above his right eye. The consequence of head-butting a large catamaran, I supposed. As with dad, I decided against bringing the subject up. It crossed my mind, though, that they made a perfect matching pair.

'Hello, Rich Uncle Brian,' I said. A safe opening gambit, without doubt. Mind you, I'd said the exact same thing when he'd picked me up at school, so I'd dropped points for originality.

'Hi, Pumpkin,' he said, clearly not taking offence. His hand moved to his trouser pocket, so I hurrumphed a little and he thought better of jingling any coins. 'You intrigue me,' he continued. 'Financial advice, eh? What's this about?'

I looked at my hamburger, which bore no resemblance to the picture over the counter. *That* burger was gorgeous. It was a pin-up burger. It gleamed. The lettuce had sparkles of fresh, pure water. The beetroot shone. The burger meat was succulent. What sat on my plate was thin pale, and resembled something you might stand on when crossing a farmer's field. I took a dim sim and thought about life's unfairness. They promise you the world [or in this case a pin-up burger] and you end up with poo. This was profound, even if I had no idea who "they" were. I wondered if profound thoughts happened often when you hit thirteen.

'You once told me you had established a trust fund for me, Rich Uncle Brian,' I said.

'Indeed I did, Pumpkin,' he replied. 'When you are twenty-one it will mature.'

'Like cheese?' I asked.

'Errr...not exactly.'

I thought about the word 'mature'. Could a trust fund behave childishly? Could it blow raspberries, chant silly rhymes and throw tantrums? Did it then find a job, get married and take out a mortgage? I shook my head. I get these kinds of thoughts a lot.

'Why?' I said.

'Why what?' said RUB. He's easily thrown by my diversions.

'Why does it mature?'

'It's a term meaning that the money is released. I want you to be able to pay off your university student loan and still have enough for a house deposit. I put money in every month.'

'Why do I have to wait until I'm twenty-one?'

Rich Uncle Brian took a bite of his burger, grimaced and wiped his chin with a napkin. Then he examined what he'd mopped up. Maybe he was thinking it would be tastier to eat the napkin.

'Well,' he replied. 'You're thirteen, Pumpkin. That's too young for important financial decisions. You could waste the cash on smart phones or computers or video games or…' He searched his imagination for other examples of wasteful purchases. '…things,' he finished lamely.

'Hello, Rich Uncle Brian!' I said. 'It's me we're talking about. Gel pens are the extent of my impulse-buying.'

'True,' he said. 'But, even so. There's significant money already invested. And if you only want to spend money on gel pens, why should there be a problem with waiting until you're twenty-one?' He said this with the air of a chess player trapping the opponent's lone King with a Queen, two Rooks and [possibly] a Bishop.

'I want to withdraw some of it.'

'I'll buy you gel pens.'

'I want fifteen thousand dollars.'

His mouth dropped open. 'Just how many gel pens do you need?' he said.

'It's not for gel pens,' I replied.

'Then what?'

So I told him.

When I finished he sat in silence. He even took a bite of his burger without thinking. He scratched his head. He screwed up his eyes. He stroked his moustache. His hand snuck into his trouser pocket, but I didn't say anything because I didn't want to disturb his train of thought. Coins jingled. Finally, he looked straight into my eyes. His expression was strange.

'What?' I said.

'Do you know what's the best thing about you, Pumpkin?' said Rich Uncle Brian finally.

'Is it that I sing my own song and dance my own dance?'

'How did you know?'

'It's something you have remarked on before,' I replied. 'The point is, will you help?'

'Of course I will, Pumpkin,' said Rich Uncle Brian. 'How could you ever doubt it?'

I finished a second dim sim. They were excellent

and probably better-tasting than a burger because they didn't have an impossible ideal to live up to.

~

Rich Uncle Brian dropped me outside the gate and I made my way to the shed. Dad sat at his computer, earphones on, lights flashing in their strange and beautiful sequence. When I tapped him on the shoulder he jumped and took off his earphones. Properly off, rather than leaving them dangling round his neck. He turned in his chair and smiled.

'Hi, Candice,' he said. 'How's it going?'

'Good,' I said. 'What are you doing?'

He glanced at his computer. 'You mean with this?'

'Nothing else I could mean.'

'I'm working on a program.'

'Pursuing a dream?'

He smiled. 'Maybe.'

'Tell me about it.'

'You don't want to know.'

'Probably not, but tell me anyway.'

He did. At length. I sat on a cardboard box while he talked. Don't ask me what it was about, okay? I know I have read the dictionary at least ten times, cover to cover, but most of the words he used were unfamiliar to me. The more he talked, the more animated he became. Excited. Involved. It was strange. I didn't understand how love for something so abstract could exist, but I knew I was witnessing it. I felt privileged. It was like sharing a glimpse into an alien yet joyous world.

'Wow,' I said when he finished. And I meant it.

Dad smiled a dreamy smile. It made him softer somehow, less angular and forbidding.

'You have no idea what I'm talking about, do you?' he said.

'Not the slightest,' I replied. 'But I meant that "Wow".'

And then, suddenly, I think I *did* get it. And it wasn't *what* Dad had said. It was the *way* he said it, his shining eyes, how he flicked his tongue in excitement as he explained. There is a brilliant word in the dictionary for what I experienced. Epiphany. Look it up. This wasn't about love for a machine. What had Dad always said? 'Anyone who can use Lego can build a computer.' The computer was a means to an end. What Dad was talking about was pure imagination. An idea. A dream he could bring to life, not with words found in a dictionary, but with source codes and algorithms [see, I have picked up *some* knowledge]. He was weaving magic and building dreams and I loved him for it.

I felt like crying, so I did.

'Candice,' said Dad. 'Why are you crying?'

'I am happy,' I said. 'What you are doing is beautiful.'

'I've never heard it described like that before,' he said. 'But thank you, Candice. That means a lot to me.'

I gurgled and blubbed. I am a messy crier.

'What about you?' he continued after my blubbing had subsided. 'What's going on in your life?'

'Douglas Benson From Another Dimension is in love with me,' I said. 'But he has solved the Earth-Pig Fish problem, so it's a fair exchange.'

'Love?' said Dad. 'Really?'

'Probably not, really,' I said. 'But there's lots of wetness involved.'

Dad seemed rather disturbed by that last statement, but recovered well. 'I don't think I've ever asked,' he said. 'But what makes you think he's from another dimension?'

'It's not what I think. It's what he believes,' I replied.

I gave Dad the whole story. I have an excellent memory, so I even threw in p-branes and M-theory and multiverses. And as I talked the most miraculous thing happened. I'd assumed Dad would be as baffled by my words as I was by his. But something passed over his expression. It was…well, it wasn't understanding. I don't think so. It was as if a switch had been flicked, a connection made, a live wire brushing and sparking against another wire. Hope lit his eyes. He grabbed a pad from his desk and made notes as I spoke. Someone writing down what you are saying is very distracting, so I dribbled to a stop. Dad didn't stop writing, however. His pen raced across the page. Finally, he slumped back in his chair, a grin plastered on his face.

'Candice,' he breathed. 'You are a genius.'

'Only a bit,' I said. 'Why?'

'Because…because you are.'

I didn't find his words convincing, but decided not to point this out. Anyway, Dad's face suddenly creased. It looked like he was on the verge of crying.

Then he slipped off the verge and did.

Mum made breakfast. Bacon and eggs and grilled mush-rooms. She moved around the kitchen with purpose, a defiant smile on her face. I watched from the corner of my eyes and every time she passed through a beam of sunlight arrowing through the kitchen window her face twitched in pain. But the smile stayed stuck. She had it pinned and nothing was going to shift it.

Dad set the table and we ate together, though Mum didn't eat much. She nibbled on a piece of toast and narrowed her eyes. Dad was also somewhere else. I could tell by his face. He asked about school, but as I replied his face glazed over. He'd nod occasionally, but he wasn't listening. He was lost in a place where no one could follow. Chasing a dream.

'I'm doing biography research in English today,' I said. 'I've been paired with Jen Marshall. We have to interview each other.'

Dad nodded, but Mum put down her toast.

'Isn't she the little…' She was searching for the right word. Or maybe an acceptable word for breakfast conversation. '…*madam* you told us about? The one with tattoos and body piercing?'

'That's her.'

Mum picked up the toast, looked at it and put it back on the plate.

'She doesn't sound like someone you'd have much in common with, Pumpkin.'

'*Au contraire*,' I replied. 'Jen Marshall has many wonderful qualities. I am confident we will become bosom buddies, or, as Jen would say, BFFs – Best Friends Forever.'

Mum seemed dubious, but that might have been the toast, which obviously didn't inspire her with confidence.

Dad nodded a couple of times. Then he broke from his trance.

'Could you ask Douglas Benson to come round for dinner tonight?' he said. 'I want to have a chat with him. I'll cook,' he added hastily in response to a frown from Mum, who had obviously not been consulted about this plan.

'He has an appointment with destiny at six-thirty every night,' I said. 'But he might be able to come round after that. I will ask.'

Dad gave another dreamy smile, which I took as a cue to head to school.

~

Miss Cowie took us to the library because the English classroom was not suitable for thirteen pairs of students talking intimately. She suggested we sit on the floor or down one of the library aisles so we could have privacy. I found this exciting and proof that Miss Cowie was an inspirational teacher, prepared to think outside the square [I've never been convinced there is a square that most people think inside, but so many people talk about it, it must be true. Why not a circle?]. Jen Marshall gazed around the library as if seeing it for the first time, which, it turned out, was true. Miss C organised us into our pairs. Jen looked me up and down, chewed her gum and rolled her eyes. For one horrible moment I thought she might have choked on her gum again, but it was okay. She just wasn't impressed with me. She looked over at her friends longingly, glanced at me and rolled her eyes again. She is a *terrific* eye-roller. Her friends giggled, pointed to their own heads and made little circles in the air. Jen rolled her eyes again. It was like a mime show and I was enjoying it, but time was marching on.

'We should start, Jen,' I said. 'Where would you like to sit?'

'Anywhere away from you, Essen,' she replied.

'Not possible, I'm afraid,' I said. 'What about down this aisle [*aisle B, reference section*]? You could talk to me and your friends won't see.'

She chewed her gum and shifted her weight onto one hip. She looked elegant, apart from the gum-chewing, which caused her mouth to open and close like Earth-Pig Fish's. It wasn't very becoming. If our interview went well, I thought I might mention it. Jen is concerned about making good impressions.

'Whaddayaonabout?' she asked.

'Well,' I said. 'It is obvious that being seen with me is embarrassing for you. Talking to me must be even more embarrassing. If we go down this aisle, we could chat, get the assignment done and your friends would never know you'd said anything to me at all.'

Jen shifted her weight onto her other hip and chewed faster. Then she glanced at her friends, rolled her eyes and took off down aisle B. I followed. Jen sat on the carpet and curled her legs beneath her. She has nice legs.

Hers are shapely whereas mine are thin and stick-like [though I suppose that's a shape in itself]. They are practical, just not pleasing on the eyes.

'Tell me about yourself, Jen,' I said.

She shrugged and glanced up and down the aisle. We were alone.

'What's to say?' she said.

'Tell me about your family.'

'Mother, drunk a lotta the time. Dad, God knows where. Brother who's a retard. No offence. What's to say?'

'Doesn't sound like a happy family life,' I ventured.

She looked at me, properly this time, and didn't roll her eyes. This was progress.

'Yeah. So what? I bet you have one of those families that you see on TV. Everyone like all loving and drooling over school reports and going on holidays and all that crap. Well, I live in the real world, Essen. It's not as pretty as the pictures.'

I had a sudden image of a photograph that Mum kept on her bedside cabinet. Mum, Dad, me and Sky, and all of us smiling. I shook my head. This was about Jen.

'What do you want to be when you leave school?' I asked.

'Are you for real? I can't think that far ahead. I just

want to get out of this crappy place, okay? It's crap, all of it. The school's crap, the teachers are crap, the lessons are crap. It's all crap.'

I felt she had communicated her attitude towards education very clearly. She thought it was crap [I must be honest here. Jen didn't use the word 'crap' but another word that I gloss over when I get to S in the dictionary].

'But you're not, Jen, are you?'

'What?'

'Crap.'

'Yeah, I am.' She seemed angry at my suggestion that she wasn't. 'I'm crap too. In fact, I'm more crap than anything else. I'm crap at schoolwork, even though that's crap. You name the subject, I'm crap at it. English, totally crap. Science? Complete crap.'

'I could help you.'

'What?' She stopped chewing. 'Whaddaya mean?'

'I could help with your homework. Don't worry, none of your friends need know. But you could come to my house, if you like. Or we could go to the library after school. I'm good at most subjects and I'm certain I could help.'

'The library?' she said. 'Yeah, right!'

Why do people say 'Yeah, right!' when they actually mean 'No, wrong!'? It's something I've thought about and I cannot work it out. Then again, I have difficulty working most things out.

'Why would you do that?' she added. Suspicion oozed from every word.

'Because I like you.'

'You're so weird, Essen,' she said. 'You *like* me? Well, I hate you. I think you are, like, the biggest…penis head [*I did it again*] in the entire crappy school. Why would you like me, huh? I treat you like crap. Because you are crap. So what is it with you? Is it, like, the worse you get treated the nicer you try to be? Mum's like that with the men she brings home. She's a loser and so are you.'

'Possibly, but I'd still like to help you with your schoolwork.'

Jen shifted uncomfortably and looked down the aisle again. We were still alone. Even so, she lowered her voice.

'Maybe,' she said. 'But only if no one ever knows. You promise, Essen? Swear that no one will ever find out. 'Cos I've got my reputation to think about.'

'I understand,' I said. 'And I promise.'

'I'm not saying I'll do it, like,' said Jen. 'But I'll think about it. That's all I'm saying.'

'I understand.'

'Doesn't mean I don't think you're crap,' she added. ''Cos I do.'

'I understand.'

'How about tomorrow tonight? You give me your address, I'll come to your place. About eight-thirty. Okay?'

'Okay.'

I wrote my address on a piece of a notepaper and handed it to her. I got the feeling she wanted to read it and then eat it, but she tucked it into her jeans pocket instead.

She left aisle B [*Reference section*] ahead of me. Out of the corners of my eyes, I saw her approach her friends. There was much eye-rolling and giggling and tracing circles in the air next to heads.

It was obvious Jen Marshall and I were bonding.

~

Douglas Benson From Another Dimension was keen to come for dinner. His facsimile dad would drop him at our place right after he'd jumped out of his tree [unless it worked this time and Douglas was spending quality time with his theoretical-physicist mother and experimental-musician father. I felt the odds were good he'd show up].

When I got home, Mum was up and watching television. As soon as I opened the door she clicked off the set and gave me a hug.

'How was your interview with Jen Marshall?' she asked.

I was impressed on all sorts of levels. She was up. She gave me a hug. She remembered what I'd been doing in school.

'All good,' I said. 'She's coming round tomorrow night, but you can't tell anyone.'

Mum seemed puzzled, but nodded.

'It's only a matter of time before we are talking sleepovers,' I added.

Mum gave the puzzled nod another airing.

'What are we doing for your birthday?' I asked. Mum's birthday was a couple of days away. I asked with little hope of getting a sensible reply, since I couldn't remember the last time we had done anything to celebrate the occasion. Most of my memories are of sneaking into her bedroom, bumping my knee on her side of the bed and handing over a wrapped present in the total darkness that I knew would be un-opened in the morning. The present, I mean. Not the darkness. But this time Mum was full of life.

'I thought we'd go to a restaurant for dinner,' she replied. 'What the hell, heh? Push the boat out. You're only forty-two once.'

'Excellent,' I said, though it occurred to me that there really *is* no way to avoid chicken parmigiana and a rendition of 'Happy Birthday To You.' Not even near-death by drowning can stop it.

Dinner was rushed on the grounds that Dad was desperate to get Douglas Benson From Another Dimension into his shed for a chat.

'I hope you'll like the food, Douglas,' he said. 'It's…'

'Sausage, egg and chips,' I said.

'How did you know?' said Dad.

'Because it's the only thing you know how to cook, Dad,' I replied. This was true. Dad had cooked probably half-a-dozen times since I was old enough to pay attention, and each time it had been sausage, egg and chips. Nutritionally, it was excellent that he spent so much time in his shed and so little in the kitchen, otherwise you'd be able to squeeze the fat out of me and use it to supply a small third-world country with lamp oil.

'You think I can't cook anything else?' said Dad, looking hurt.

'I do,' I said.

'That's unkind, Candice.'

'It's honest.'

'Sausage, egg and chips is great, Mr Phee,' said Douglas Benson From Another Dimension, with the air of someone trying to get on the right side of a future father-in-law. Actually, it's funny that this thought occurred to me because fifteen minutes later, as I was finishing my egg [I like to finish the egg before I start on the sausages] Douglas dropped the following into the conversation:

'I would like to marry your daughter, Mr Phee. With your blessing, of course.'

Dad was halfway through chewing a piece of sausage. He spluttered, choked and spat the sausage at speed over the table, where it landed in Mum's water glass and bobbed about unpleasantly. To be fair to Mum, she fished it out with a napkin and a minimum of fuss.

'Excuse me?' said Dad.

'I love Candice.'

'Er, she's thirteen, Douglas. *Just* thirteen. Do you not think that's a little on the young side?'

'I don't mean right now, Mr Phee.'

'Oh, good.'

'Maybe in three or four years' time.'

'And what do you bring to the table, Douglas?' said Dad, after a long silence [though I might have heard a stifled giggle from Mum].

'I beg your pardon, Mr Phee?'

'A herd of goats? A flock of sheep, maybe? I'm not sure I could let her go for less than two buffalo and a couple of suckling pigs.'

Douglas Benson From Another Dimension scratched the knobbly bits on his head.

'Wow, Dad,' I said. 'I didn't know you were funny.'

Mum washed up while Douglas and I followed Dad to the shed. Dad spent forty-five minutes grilling Douglas on every aspect of other dimensions. It was a subject that Douglas was much more comfortable with than marriage proposals, and he answered with enthusiasm. I didn't understand why Dad was asking. I also didn't understand why he was getting more and more excited.

I got the answer after Douglas's facsimile father picked him up and Dad and I were alone. He told me about his new project. Though I didn't understand most of the technical details, I knew it was brilliant. Some things you can just *feel*. Unfortunately, he made me promise not to speak to anyone about it.

And I never break my promises.

Dear Denille,

   I am excited and I will explain.
To start with, here is a line:

   Forget about the line. That's not what
I'm excited about. Just answer this: What
is it that everyone in the world is obsessed
with? While you are thinking that one
through, here is another diagram:

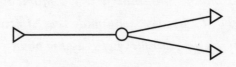

Got the answer?

It's YOURSELF!

This is the way Dad explained it. Why are social networking sites so popular? Why do reality television programs rate so highly? Why does everyone post videos on YouTube (I'm not exactly sure what YouTube is, but I hear about it at school and Dad was quite excited about it and I was carried along with his enthusiasm)? The answer is…people want to feel they are important, that the Earth revolves around them. It is, according to Dad, like staring into a mirror, not caring that the world is going on without you.

So, what have the lines got to do with it? Good question. Think of that first line as representing your life – a timeline from birth to where you are now. We think of it as a line because we can trace the path clearly. It is all the moments we have lived and it runs straight because we have not deviated from our life (duh, obviously). But what about the life we might have led? Look at the branch in that second line and think of it as a moment in life when a decision was made that affected you. Here's an example: Let's say the point

where the branch occurs is when you were two
and your parents had another child. If they
hadn't, your life would have gone along one
of the arrows on the line, but if they did, then
your life goes along the other line. What if
your father or mother had been offered a job
that meant he or she had to move to another
country? In this life, he/she turned it down. But
if he/she had accepted, then your life would
have changed enormously. You would have
different friends, have gone to a different
school, maybe have learned another language.
Then think how just a few decisions, big and
small, might have changed you. Your possible
life. Then the line looks something like this:

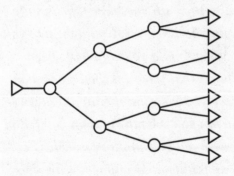

You see? After only three decisions, there
are eight possible lives. Now think of ALL
the decisions made, not just big ones, but

small ones as well. The answer is clear.
There are an infinite number of possible
lives that might have been, though you
are only aware of the one you are living.

Now, this is where Douglas Benson
From Another Dimension comes in. You see,
his explanation of alternative dimensions
is close to this. According to him, there
is an infinity of worlds in which an
infinity of possibilities are played out.

What fun, Denille!

And now I get to the heart of the matter.
Our obsession with ourselves. The infinity of
possible lives. Dad put it like this: Imagine
a computer program, Candice, that allowed
you to alter the path you have taken in life
by changing decisions inside and outside your
control. What would your life have been
like? What if that program then created an
alternative you (or a number of alternative
yous) based upon the information you fed in
and allowed you to communicate with her?
A multi-dimensional social media site where
you could interact with as many yous as you
wished. You could see how you might have
looked, you could view pictures of the children

you might have had, watch videos of holidays
you might have gone on, share in the glorious
successes and failures that were denied you in
this life. And you could talk to yourself, post
messages, get replies. You could explore the full
potential of your existence, not just plod along
the path you are trapped on. How many of us
have wondered what would have happened
if we had only done this, or not done that? All
of us! This program would allow you to find
out. Why should we be content with one life
when there is an infinite number available?

'And could you write that program, Dad?'
I asked.

'Yes,' he said. 'I could. It would be
enormously complicated for one person to do
and it would need a significant amount of
investment, start-up capital and the like. But
yes, I can do it, though it will take years.'

It's such a simple idea, Denille, but also
exciting, even for someone like me who can't
find a computer's on button. What would my
life have been like if Sky hadn't died or if Mum
hadn't got breast cancer or if Dad and Rich
Uncle Brian hadn't argued? Now, I know it's
theoretically a fiction – the alternative yous

would be created by the computer program. But people love fiction. And if Douglas Benson From Another Dimension is to be believed, it's not truly fiction, since whatever the program does is happening in an alternative universe anyway. It would be a real glimpse into a real world.

I found this so amazing that I thought knobbly bits would break out on my head, but they didn't. So there you have it, Denille. My father's dream. And do you know something? It's as if he has lost years in the space of a few days. He smiles (dreamily) and it suits him. I am getting back the father I'd almost forgotten existed. My alternative father.

Okay, I had better stop here.

Please don't tell anyone or write to them about this idea, Denille. According to my Dad it could be worth billions of dollars, but that's not really important. It's Dad's idea and it would be horrible if someone stole it. In fact, I promised I wouldn't speak to anyone about it, but, as you can tell, I haven't.

I have written it down. No speaking involved.

Anyway, you are my third-best friend in the whole world (after Douglas Benson

From Another Dimension and Earth-
Pig Fish) and I trust you absolutely.
    Best wishes,
    Your penpal,
    Candice

~

Suddenly my life had become very exciting, what with Mum having a proper birthday, Dad following his dreams [and talking to me about them] and Earth-Pig Fish finding an atheist perspective on life.

The following day was no less exciting. Firstly, Rich Uncle Brian met me at school and handed me a plastic card worth fifteen thousand dollars. It didn't look like it was worth that much, but I know as much about banking as I do about computers, so I just accepted the situation. And the card.

Douglas Benson From Another Dimension came with me to the library at lunchtime. I needed him to help me with some online research and purchasing, and he thought there might be a kiss in it for him. While the signs on the walls are clear about eating and drinking, there was nothing about kissing [which might be a serious omission]; however, I suspected the librarians, who are generally tolerant of my eating [and my personal chair], might frown at snogging, and I told Douglas this. We spent all lunchtime huddled over a computer until I had made my choice and paid for it [Douglas operated the mouse and clicked all the links].

'I've got exciting news, Candice,' he said as we headed towards Maths.

'All news is exciting at the moment,' I replied.

'I think I know where I have been going wrong.'

I thought he might be referring to proposing to a thirteen-year-old in front of her parents, but I was mistaken.

'It's the nature of the tesseract,' he continued. 'I think I have made a serious error with one of the dimensions. It would explain everything. And if I'm right, then there is no reason why I shouldn't return to my own dimension.'

'That *is* exciting,' I said. 'When are you going to try?'

'I need to check the maths fully. That will take a few days. Once I'm certain, then I'll probably go back on Sunday.'

'That is a good day to cross dimensions,' I said, though I have no idea why. Sometimes you need to say *something*.

'Will you watch me?' he said. 'I know it might sound insensitive, given I could be leaving you forever. But it's important to me. Will you, Candice? Please?'

How could I refuse to watch my best friend jump out of a tree on a Sunday?

'I will be there, Douglas Benson From Another Dimension,' I said. He looked delighted, but he didn't try to kiss me. That was probably sensible, since we had entered the classroom and our Maths teacher would undoubtedly disapprove. Mr Gemmola disapproves of everything except differential equations.

There was a knock on the front door at eight-thirty that evening and I opened it [Mum had gone for a lie down and Dad was in his shed, making a start]. I was expecting Jen Marshall.

Instead I got an ape. An ape in a balaclava and a black trench coat. This was, not surprisingly, alarming. It was even more alarming when the ape barged me to one side, rushed into the house and slammed the door behind it. It is possible you have never experienced having your house invaded by an ape in a balaclava, but take my word, it is definitely alarming. The ape raised a hand to its face and ripped off first the balaclava and then what turned out to be a latex mask.

'Hello, Jen Marshall,' I said. 'You look nice.'

'Did you see anyone behind me, Essen?' she hissed.

'The door was open for half a second, Jen. And I was so focused on the ape mask I didn't look over its…your…shoulder,' I said. 'Is this a fancy-dress themed homework session?' I added.

'You should've seen the looks I got on the bus,' she

said. 'But I wasn't taking no chances, Essen. If anyone had seen me come here, then I'd a been…'

'An outcast?' I suggested.

'Whatever,' she replied. 'Let's get this done, okay? I don't want to miss the last bus, 'cos I can't walk home in an ape costume, can I? There are weirdoes out there.'

But not many dressed as King Kong, I thought.

'What's the assignment?' I said.

'It's crap,' she said. 'Soc. Ed., which is, like, a really crap subject. And this is a crap assignment for a crap subject and I'm crap at it.'

'Let's scrape away some crap, shall we?' I suggested. 'Do you want me to hang up your ape mask?'

IS FOR WITNESS

Thursday.

Mum's birthday was on Friday [tomorrow], but I had everything arranged apart from the card. Dad had booked a table at a local restaurant. I asked him what he had bought Mum and he showed me a brooch in the shape of a bird. It might have been a parrot. I am not expert in the identification of birdlife, so I won't swear to it.

'I've got her something else,' he said. 'But it's a surprise. Actually, I'm worried how she will react to it. I guess I'll find out tomorrow. And what have you bought her, Candice? If you need to borrow money, by the way...'

'Thanks, Dad,' I replied, 'but I'm okay.' Actually, I only had twenty-two dollars, but that was enough for an amusing card that poked fun at middle-aged people. In the meantime I had two days of school to get through. It turned out they were interesting.

Not as interesting as the weekend that followed, though.

English was after lunch. I really hoped Miss Bamford was back. For one thing, I was worried about her. What if she had some life-threatening illness? Maybe she was, even now, in a hospital ward recovering from an operation and in desperate need of a cheery visit from her favourite student [Miss B has never spoken openly of this, but I am a good judge of character and know she holds me in high regard]. I could make her laugh. Without trying, apparently.

But I was also worried about me. I am a creature of habit and routine. Miss Cowie was obviously a talented teacher [though not as good, clearly, as Miss Bamford, who – I think I might have mentioned this – is the best teacher in the whole world *as far as I am concerned*], but I knew it was oral presentation time today and I didn't know if I could speak in front of her. So I had spent time in the library writing a note.

~

Dear Miss Cowie,

*I am Candice Phee. Maybe Miss Bamford
has mentioned me. If she hasn't, there are
a couple of things you should know. I have
an ex-dysfunctional fish and a pernickety
pencil case, with a divider so my pencils
don't get mixed up. I always have to sit in
the same seat. I don't talk to people until
I feel comfortable with them. This sometimes
takes weeks. In the meantime I communicate
through notes like this one. Some people
think I am on some sort of spectrum, but
I don't think I am. It's just that I am different
from most students. I know all students are
different, but I am more different than most.*

*Now, you strike me as a person who also
has routines and I imagine making eye-contact
during an oral presentation is something you
require. Please don't make me do this, Miss
Cowie, as I will suffer from severe anxiety.
I will also have to read from a prepared
speech which I know is not ideal. I will quite
understand if you fail me because of this, but
I would fail anyway if you made me speak
without a script because I wouldn't be able to.*

Very best wishes,
Candice Phee

P.S. I very much admire your refusal to read newspapers, knit, surf the internet or build plastic models while we are working.

P.P.S. I am not, as some students in this class would say, trying to be a 'brown nose' (mine just peels in the sun anyway). I am sincere and like you very much.

P.P.P.S. Is there any news about Miss Bamford? I miss her. Thank you.

~

Miss Cowie sat at her desk with a back so straight bricklayers could have used it for a plumbline [I read about this in an encyclopaedia – the plumbline, I mean, not Miss Cowie's back]. As I shuffled past I placed the note in front of her and quickly sat at my desk. I kept my head down so I had no idea if she'd read it or simply screwed it up and thrown it in the bin. She certainly gave the impression of someone who would screw up notes without a second thought. The class sat in silence for a minute.

'It is oral presentation time, class,' said Miss Cowie finally. 'Now I know some of you are nervous about speaking in front of your peers, so I should stress that this is practice only. When Miss Bamford returns – and I believe that will be tomorrow – she will doubtless have her own ideas about the oral assessment. So today, if you wish, you can read prepared speeches or use notes or simply talk without any aids. Relax and do your best. That's all I ask.'

I was so surprised that I glanced up as she paced between our desks. She bent down to pick up some litter next to my seat and, as she straightened, gave me a long, slow wink.

Miss Cowie is the second-best teacher in the world [*as far as I am concerned*].

The second-best teacher in the world [*as far as I am concerned*] returned to her desk, sat down and examined her roll.

'The first pair to present will be Candice Phee and Jennifer Marshall. Candice, would you like to start, please?'

I got to my feet, opened my English book and cleared my throat. I could hear giggles from the back of the class. Jen's friends, presumably, but they quickly shut up when Miss Cowie, I imagined, did a steely routine with her eyes. I kept my head over my book.

'Jennifer Marshall is beautiful,' I read. 'That much is obvious when you look at her. She has wonderful hair, a delightful complexion and legs to die for. But that is not all that Jen Marshall is. Physical beauty is an accident, often not earned. But Jen is also a beautiful person on the inside. We simply need to look closely and carefully to see it. Her life has not been easy. I could give details, but this is not the time or place. So I suppose you will have to take my word for it. Jen has suffered. Under these circumstances, some people would become angry. They might despise the world. They might give up on themselves.'

The class was deadly quiet. The silence was a dark pressure and I could feel sweat stand on my forehead. I ploughed on.

'But Jen has not. She tries to improve herself. She understands her weaknesses and works to improve them. If I have any criticism of Jennifer Marshall, it is that she lacks self-confidence. She thinks she is not worthy. She cannot see what the rest of us see so easily – that underneath that beautiful exterior is a beautiful person. One thing is clear. Jennifer Marshall is an exceptional person. She will become an exceptional adult. It is my dearest wish that, one day, I may call her my best friend. Thank you.'

I sat down, which was wise since my legs were on the point of folding. I busied myself with putting my English book back in its proper place on the desk and tidying my pernickety pencil case. Nonetheless, I heard the applause from the rest of the class. It sounded genuine, though I could, of course, be mistaken. It is difficult, in my experience, to distinguish between false applause and genuine applause. They sound very much the same. Anyway, when the clapping died, I heard Miss Cowie.

'Well, Candice. Thank you. Rather short on facts and details, but a heartfelt response. Well done. Jennifer, your turn.'

I didn't look up. There was shuffling and then a long silence.

'Er...okay.' Jen sounded terrified. 'Yeah. Well. Candice Phee. Right. Okay. So. Candice Phee. She's special needs, and no mistake.' There were a couple of giggles, stifled immediately. Silence returned. 'But she's okay, is Candice. Yeah. Thanks.'

I didn't hear what Miss Cowie had to say about Jen's oral presentation. I could probably guess.

But I thought it was brilliant.

~

Douglas Benson From Another Dimension walked me home after school. He insisted on holding my hand all the way, even though it was warm and after a while it was like gripping a dishcloth. He didn't seem to notice. They say love is blind.

'Would you like to come round for lunch on Sunday,

Candice? It might be our last opportunity to spend quality time together, especially if I'm leaving for good at six-thirty.'

Here is one thing that's really great about Douglas Benson From Another Dimension: he is so weird he makes me seem normal.

Maybe not.

But if he's not proposing to me over dinner, he's planning to vanish from the world forever. I am confused by this. True love and vanishing don't go together in any conventional sense. I do love the knobbly bits on his head [and his eyebrows are spectacular], but are these a solid foundation for marriage? If your husband is living in another dimension [albeit with knobbly bits on his head and spectacular eyebrows], won't this put undue pressure on the relationship?

What would our children be like? It doesn't bear thinking about.

'That sounds good, Douglas,' I said.

We arranged for me to be there at two in the afternoon. We'd have a late lunch with the facsimile parents, visit the ravine and then gather round the tree-portal. Well, I'd gather [can one person gather? Is that physically possible?] while Douglas found an appropriate branch.

If his attempt succeeded … well, that would be that.

If it failed, we'd probably discuss wedding arrangements with the facsimile parents. I couldn't decide which would be the weirder outcome.

When we reached my house, Rich Uncle Brian was waiting outside in his car. This was something I had arranged. Douglas said a reluctant goodbye and I got into the front seat of RUB's four-wheel drive. We drove off. We did not visit a fast food eatery for a burger of dubious origin. Not this time. We drove to a supermarket car park and parked. Rich Uncle Brian did some reading [I provided the material] and I did some humming [I provided this too]. Then we talked briefly and he drove me home.

We know how to have a good time, me and Rich Uncle Brian.

I still had the finer details to arrange, but everything was coming together nicely. It is true that family harmony had not been restored by my first plan. Indeed, throwing myself into the ocean had only made our problems worse. But Candice Phee does *not* give up.

This time, I thought. This time.

IS FOR XENOPHOBIA

[or lack thereof ... look it up in the dictionary]

'Happy Birthday, Mum,' I said. 'You don't look a day over forty-two.'

'Thanks, Pumpkin. Thanks a lot.' But she smiled when she said it.

Dad cooked breakfast on Friday morning. I peered into the frying pan. It was sausages and eggs. Dad glanced at me.

'What?' he said. 'It's a versatile dish, Candice. Breakfast, lunch, dinner. Just add or subtract chips. We five-star chefs have learned to experiment. You wouldn't understand. It's called haute cuisine.'

'You can't do bacon?'

'I'm working my way up to bacon. It might take a year or two.'

This all felt strange. We had gone from misery to sit-com dialogue in a matter of days. I knew Dad was right when he'd told me there would be good days and bad days. I decided that before it had only been bad days, so I'd settle for this.

'Do you want your presents now, Mum?' I asked.

Mum toyed with a sausage and then nibbled at the corner of her toast.

'No, thanks,' she replied. 'Your dad and I thought it would be good to do presents at dinner tonight.'

'Can you wait that long?'

'I'm forty-two, Pumpkin. Trust me, the waiting is easy.' She took a white tablet and swallowed it with a sip of water. Then she noticed me noticing. 'Happy pills, Candice. And you know something? They might be working.'

'I'm happy,' I said.

'You know something else, Pumpkin? I might be getting to that place myself.'

~

Total silence greeted the entrance of Miss Bamford into our English classroom at first lesson.

It wasn't the shock of her return. It was the black

eye patch she was wearing. Oh, and the rubber parrot fixed to her left shoulder. She stood for a moment in front of her desk and gazed at our sea of faces.

'Would anyone care to take this black spot to Blind Pugh?' she growled.

This must have been a joke, but I don't think anyone got it. We just stared. Then someone at the back of the class laughed. Someone else joined in. Before we knew it, everyone was laughing, especially Miss Bamford. I had never known such a day of laughter and it was only nine in the morning.

Miss B eventually removed the parrot, which was a pity because it suited her. She kept the eye patch on. After the class calmed down we got to work reading our shared novel, a story about a girl, a red-haired boy and their nasty English teacher. It was okay, but it certainly wasn't Dickens. When the bell rang I stayed behind.

'Ah, Candice,' said Miss Bamford. 'How have you got on while I've been away? Not too stressful?'

'A bit, Miss. I'm glad you're back.'

'Me too, Candice.'

'Why *were* you off school, Miss?'

She sat on the edge of a desk and touched the corner of her eye patch with one finger.

'I had an operation on my lazy eye, Candice. It was a nerve-racking yet straightforward procedure tightening up a few muscles. Now you wouldn't know I'd ever had a problem.'

'It must be badly bruised, Miss. Lots of swelling?'

'What makes you think that?'

'The eye patch.'

'Oh, that.' She lifted the patch and I saw her eye. It was clear. And straight. There was no bruising at all. Her face looked perfect. 'The patch was your present, Candice. Wearing it is *my* present to you.'

'It's a lovely present,' I said. 'And I'm glad I helped you get your eye fixed.'

'Sorry?' said Miss Bamford.

'Our discussion when I gave you the patch. You must have immediately booked the operation.'

Miss Bamford smiled.

'Well, not *quite*, Candice. The operation was arranged over eighteen months ago. There's a very long waiting list.'

I have to confess I was disappointed. A coincidence only? I am a firm believer in honesty. I hope that has been clear throughout these chapters. But sometimes honesty can be…painful. Miss Bamford must have noticed my expression because she touched me gently on the shoulder.

'Go on, girl.' She shooed me away. 'You are going to be late for your next lesson.'

I got to the door, but she stopped me.

'Candice?' she said. I turned. 'What do you think, then? Does it make me look sinister, romantic, mysterious?'

I smiled. 'All three, Miss.'

'Oh, and another thing. The Alphabet Autobiography?'

'Nearly there, Miss Bamford,' I said. 'Nearly there.'

~

We dressed in our best clothes and drove to the restaurant. I wore a dress with a floral print that I saved for special occasions. Eight dollars at the Albright op-shop. Money has been tight the last few years, but we make it stretch.

The owner of the restaurant greeted us personally.

'G'day Jim, Vicky, Candice,' he said. 'Great to see youse guys.'

'Hey, Scot. Howya going?'

'Fit as a butcher's dog, mate. Table for three is it?'

'Please.'

We hadn't been to the restaurant since my twelfth birthday, but Albright is that kind of place. Everyone knows everyone. Most of the time, that's nice.

We sat at a table near the window where we could see the river, and Scot brought us menus.

'What's good tonight, Scot?' asked Dad.

'The chicken parmigiana is flying off the counter, mate.'

'You should have killed the chicken first, then,' said Mum.

Scot cocked his hand and pointed a finger at Mum.

'Good one, Vick. Good one. Listen, guys, you want drinks while you make up yer minds?'

'You got champagne, Scot?' asked Dad.

'Course, mate. What's the celebration?'

'It's my birthday,' said Mum.

'Congrats,' said Scot. 'So how old then, Vick? Twenty-four? Twenty-five?'

'Ah, get away with you, Scot,' said Mum. 'My mind says twenty-five, but my body says much, much older.'

'Trust yer mind, then,' said Scot. 'So, what type of champers then? We got everything from Dom Pérignon at one-sixty a bottle to something slightly more…Australian, at thirty-five.'

We took the thirty-five dollar bottle. And the chicken parmigiana. That was the cheapest on the menu as well. But it was all good [I can't swear to the champagne. I had orange juice]. When we'd finished, Scot brought out a birthday cake with four candles on it [Dad must have given the restaurant a heads-up]. Scot said he couldn't put on the correct number of candles, because there were laws about fire hazards in restaurants. Mum slapped his wrist, squealed and blew out the candles while all the customers and staff sang 'Happy Birthday To You.' Most people sang through mouthfuls of chicken parmigiana and the effect was muffled but impressive.

Albright is that kind of place.

Then Scot brought out another bottle of champagne – an expensive one this time [there was French writing on the label] – and placed it in an ice bucket next to our table. 'On the house,' he said. 'Happy birthday, darl.'

Albright is that kind of place.

'We can't drink all that grog, Scot,' said my Dad. 'I mean, thanks, but I've got to drive.'

'Nah,' said Scot. 'All arranged, mate. I'm driving you home and me wife'll drive your car back.'

Albright is that kind of place.

Dad refilled their glasses and pulled out a small, wrapped package.

'Happy birthday, Vicky,' he said, passing it over.

Mum's eyes shone as she opened it. 'Oh, Jim,' she said. 'It's lovely. A kookaburra brooch.'

'I thought it was a galah,' said Dad.

'It's a parrot,' I said.

Whatever it was, Mum pinned it on and Dad took a photograph. Then it was my turn. I gave Mum the card first. It said something about how you know you're middle-aged when your narrow hips and your broad mind switch places. Mum found it funny. Or pretended to.

'I have four presents for you, Mum,' I said.

'Goodness, Candice,' she said. 'Four?'

'Well, three go together to make one big one and the other is a piece of information, which explains why it's not gift-wrapped.'

'Information?'

'Yes. It's fascinating.'

'I'm all ears.'

'Not entirely,' I said. 'Anyway, here it is. Most people think chicken parmigiana is an Italian dish, named after the Italian city of Parma. But you can't find chicken parmigiana anywhere in Italy. They've never heard of it.'

'That *is* fascinating,' said Mum. 'It is a gift I will treasure.'

'You are being ironic,' I said. 'Possibly sarcastic. But it is your birthday and you are entitled.'

'Those Italians don't know what they're missing,' said Dad. He patted his belly. 'That parmigiana was delicious.'

'Yes, but you think sausage and eggs is haute cuisine,' I pointed out.

'Only when it's with chips,' he said.

Mum smiled.

'Time for my second gift,' Dad said. He took from his jacket pocket a large envelope, curled into a cylinder, and handed it to Mum. He seemed worried. His smile was tight and he pulled at his earlobe. Mum tore it open [the envelope, not Dad's earlobe], removed a document and tilted her head to one side. The silence stretched.

'I don't understand, Jim,' she said finally. 'What is it?'

'A star,' he said. 'That is the official certificate of ownership. There is another document in there which shows you a picture of the star system, with your star circled.'

'How can you buy a star?' asked Mum.

'On the internet,' said Dad. 'This particular star is about two hundred light years away.'

I thought this was incredibly exciting. You see, Douglas Benson From Another Dimension had explained light years to me one lunchtime. We had been in the library, though I hadn't had a sandwich. The whole concept was mind-boggling. Well, my mind had boggled. I was confident Mum's mind would boggle too.

'Mum,' I said. 'A light year is the distance light travels in a year. Now, light travels at about three hundred thousand kilometres a second. That's eighteen million kilometres a minute, over a billion kilometres an hour.'

'Goodness,' said Mum.

'Goodness, indeed,' I replied. 'So if your star is two hundred light years away, it's easy to work out the distance. Over one billion times twenty-four hours in a day is over twenty-four billion kilometres. There are three hundred and sixty-five days in a year [we will ignore leap years], so…twenty four billion multiplied by three hundred and sixty-five, which is…' Where was Mr Gemmola when you needed him? 'A very, very long way,' I finished. 'Very,' I added, just in case she'd missed the point. 'Very. If you got into your van and tried to drive to it…'

'I'd need extra jerry cans,' finished Dad.

'And serious commitment to additional road building by the Queensland government,' said Mum.

'I should tell you, Vicky,' said Dad. 'The ownership document is essentially meaningless. Official Astronomical Societies around the world don't recognise it. They have their own classifications and don't name stars. It's really a symbol.'

'This is named?' said Mum.

'Yes. That's what the certificate does.'

'You've named it after me?'

'Not quite,' said Dad. He pulled out the bottle of champagne and filled his glass. He didn't bother with Mum's. His fingers pulled at an ear again.

'Not *quite*?' asked Mum.

'I've named it Frances Phee. So now, every time we look at the stars we'll... well, we'll know she's there.'

There was a silence. It was one of those that can go either way. To tears or laughter. I held my breath.

'I know where she is, Jim,' said Mum.

'Yes,' said Dad. 'I know. I just thought... never mind. Maybe it was a bad idea.'

'I think it's a beautiful idea, Dad,' I chipped in. 'Because I don't think Sky is there in that cemetery. I think she's...'

'Enough!' said Mum. She put the certificate down on the table, but I noticed she avoided the pool of condensation from the water glasses. 'I'm not sure I can... handle this. Not right now.'

'Look...' said Dad.

'My turn,' I said. 'My three presents that go into one.'

I rummaged around in my backpack [I was organised, though it *did* look strange against my floral print dress] and passed her a photograph, a plastic card and an envelope. Envelopes were popular birthday gifts this year. She looked at the photograph first.

'It's a lovely room, Candice,' she said. 'That is a beautiful chandelier. *Two* beautiful chandeliers!'

'They're yours,' I said. 'Well, not forever. Only for a week in October. It's a picture of a suite in a New Orleans hotel, just off Bourbon Street. In the envelope are three tickets for the flights, and the card contains two thousand dollars spending money.'

I expected a strong reaction to that.

I got it.

~

Dear Denille,

We are coming to New Orleans for a week! I know New York is a long way from New Orleans, but perhaps you could come for a visit. We would be delighted to see you. We could eat jambalaya and listen to jazz. I'm hoping restaurants there don't serve chicken parmigiana (or sausage and eggs) because Dad would undoubtedly miss out on authentic Cajun cuisine.

I won't bore you with the details, but I handed over the tickets to Mum at a restaurant in Albright tonight (maybe we should rename it New Albright. American cities always seem to be New Something and there are plenty of parts of Albright that are looking shabby). She and Dad got very angry at first and told me they couldn't accept them. Dad said he smelled the hand of Rich Uncle Brian in this. Mum said it was too expensive, that I was thirteen and couldn't spend thousands of dollars on her.

But she had the tickets in her hand and excitement in her eyes.

She has always wanted to go to New Orleans, Denille, and she knew this was her only chance. I could feel it. Anyway, I tried to talk them round. I pointed out:
– That the tickets were non-refund-
   able, so it would be dumb to waste
   them on a matter of principle;
– That Rich Uncle Brian had tried to talk
   me out of it as well, but I had insisted (and
   he can never say no to me. Not really.);
– That it was my money and I could spend
   it on what I wanted. And I wanted this.

So, it is easy to guess what happened when I put all these arguments forward in my normal persuasive fashion.

They still refused to go.

Mum got all teary and Dad got all angry and they said it wasn't going to happen. There was talk of confronting Rich Uncle Brian and telling him a few home truths.

But we are going. They just don't know it yet.

By the way, I checked on Earth-Pig Fish and Skullcap-Fish before I went to sleep and they seem content, so I believe Douglas Benson From Another Dimension has indeed solved the problem. Oops. I've just remembered I haven't told you about Earth-Pig and Skullcap. This is part of the problem, Denille. Everything is changing. Trips to America (it's happening. Make an entry in your diary), computer programs involving multiple dimensions, eye patches on teachers and sundry other things have resulted in me neglecting you.

I promise to be better at writing and hope you can forgive me.

Best wishes,

Your penpal,

Candice

IS FOR YELLING

The excitement must have been too much for Mum, because she didn't rise from her bed on Saturday. Dad warned me to be quiet. I pointed out I couldn't do noisy if I tried.

I went with him to the shed and watched while he did things on his computer. He didn't put on his earphones and he chatted while he worked. It was funny. Since I'd given New Orleans as a present to Mum, he hadn't smiled. But as soon as he sat in front of his computer, a smile appeared and never left his face. Each tap on the keyboard was a small song of joy.

'Mum isn't depressed about her birthday presents, is she?' I asked.

'No, Candice,' said Dad. 'Not at all. Absolutely not. Not in a fit.'

'That means "yes", doesn't it?'

Dad put a hand in the air and wiggled it from side to side. 'She's still in shock, I think. You pulled a big surprise, kiddo. But it's not about that. It's this illness – it comes and goes and there's no rhyme nor reason to it. She's having a bad day today, but tomorrow may be different. Does that make sense?'

'No,' I said. 'But I suppose you'd have to be depressed to really understand.'

'Exactly.'

'We *are* going to New Orleans though, Dad.'

He stopped smiling then.

'Candice, I'm sorry, but we are not. This is not open for negotiation either. We appreciate the gesture, but it's not happening. I'm sorry.'

'It is.'

Dad sighed and turned back to his computer.

'How's the program going?' I said.

Dad swivelled in his chair and stroked his chin with two fingers.

'Think of the Great Wall of China,' he said. 'I reckon I've laid the first brick.'

'Dad?'

'Hmmm?'

'I know you've got a billion bricks to lay, but would you take me out for lunch today? Just the two of us? There is a fast food eatery I know that does burgers of dubious origin.'

I could see Dad struggling with the idea and not because of the bricks. I didn't know how expensive the birthday meal had been, but I did know we'd have to cut costs for a couple of weeks to pay for it. This had happened before. After my tenth birthday [I got *lots* of gel pens that year] we'd eaten virtually the same meal every day for a month. Mince and mashed potato. Mince and rice. Cottage pie. I like mince, but even I got sick of it. So I understood that money was in short supply. But I had also given them a present worth fifteen thousand dollars. Well, I'd tried. How could Dad say no to lunch after that?

'Sure, Candice,' he said. I could almost hear him mentally working out the finances. 'That would be fun. We could discuss your wedding plans. How many bridesmaids you want, the floral arrangements, that kind of thing.'

'I think I preferred it when you weren't funny,' I said.

'Really?'

'No,' I said. 'Not really.'

I was leading Dad into an ambush and I felt guilty. So I left him to his computer and went to talk it over with Earth-Pig Fish and Skullcap-Fish. I needed constructive and unbiased advice. Fish are good at that.

Does motive matter when you are about to interfere in something that isn't your business? I had already achieved a fair amount. Okay, Mum might not be cured, but her good days were becoming more frequent. Dad was a different person. He made jokes. He had purpose. We were going on a family holiday, despite all the evidence to the contrary. It felt like my family was returning. Slowly, true, but returning. I'd even helped Miss Bamford [I'm not sure if I believe in coincidences. They seem too…coincidental]. Jen Marshall had defied friends and expectations. Chalk another one up for Candice Phee.

I was on a roll. Like a gambler who cannot resist risking everything on another throw of the dice.

I put all this to Earth-Pig Fish and Skullcap-Fish. They swam their circles. *Go with the flow*, they seemed to say. *What goes around, comes around.*

We'd read a play by Shakespeare last term and there was a line that went something like this: *I am stepped in blood so far that to go back would be as tedious as to go o'er.* I felt the same way. I might as well carry on. Not that I was covered in blood.

Not yet, anyway.

~

We arrived at the fast food eatery at exactly twelve-thirty. It's a place where waiters come to take your order at the table, but Dad paused at the counter to check the pictures.

'Wow,' he said. 'That burger looks *really* good. I reckon I'll have that.'

I might have warned him, but sometimes it's important to make your own mistakes. In any event, it was unlikely he'd be eating too much, even if chicken parmigiana with a side order of sausage, egg and chips was on the menu. It wasn't, incidentally.

We found a booth by the window and Dad slid onto the bench. I slid in next to him.

'You don't want to sit opposite, Candice?' he asked.

'No thank you,' I said.

'But I'll get a crick in my neck talking to you.'

'That's fine.'

'For you, maybe.' But he didn't say anything else. We picked up the menus folded into the napkin dispenser and looked at options.

While our heads were lowered, Rich Uncle Brian slid into the bench opposite Dad.

Uh, oh!

Dad glanced up and did a double-take. His face flushed. Think of a clear summer's day and then think of storm clouds boiling up over the horizon, filling the sky. Imagine that happening in the space of a-second-and-a-half. It was touch and go whether his head would explode.

'What the hell?' he spluttered [actually, he didn't say 'hell']. If it wasn't such a tense situation I'd have been interested in Dad's body language. The muscles in his arms flinched. He half-stood, but the table stopped him. He glared at Rich Uncle Brian like he couldn't believe what he was seeing. Then he glanced at me. If looks could kill, I would have curled up and kicked my legs. Briefly. 'What the hell?' he repeated.

'Hello, Jim,' said Rich Uncle Brian.

'Let me out, Candice,' said Dad. 'We're going.'

'No,' I said. 'We're staying.'

For a moment, I thought blocking Dad in wasn't going to work. It seemed likely he would simply barge me out of my seat. I gripped the edge of the table and made like an immovable object. But Dad sat down again.

'Are you ready to order?' asked a young girl with blonde hair and pimples, unaware she was standing on the edge of an erupting volcano. Notebook and pen were poised. When there was no response, she looked up, took in Dad's expression and tucked the pen behind one ear. 'I'll give you more time,' she added, and bustled away, maybe to call the cops. Dad's face had gone beyond storm and was approaching hurricane.

'Is this your doing, Candice?' he growled.

I nodded.

'Let me out.'

I shook my head.

'We need to talk, Jim,' said Rich Uncle Brian.

'We have nothing to say.'

'I think we do.'

'What you think is of no interest to me. Leave. Now.'

'I want to talk about your program. The multi-dimensional social media idea.'

There's storm. Then there's hurricane. What's beyond that? I have no idea, but Dad reached it within half a second. He turned to me, as if not believing what his ears were telling him. He'd mentioned this to no one. Except me. But I could tell he was searching for some other explanation. Anything, no matter how fanciful, that wouldn't mean betrayal by his own daughter. He couldn't find it. I saw it in his face.

'Candice?' he said. His voice was low and pain-filled. It would have been better if he'd shouted.

'I didn't speak about it, Dad,' I said. 'I wrote it down and showed it to Rich Uncle Brian. I didn't break my promise.'

'What?'

'You told me not to speak about it to anyone. I haven't. But you didn't say anything about letting someone read it.' There was a pause. 'I'm literal, Dad. You know that.'

'You are also smart, Candice,' he said. 'So don't play the "literal" card. You knew how important this was to me and now you've ruined it. It wouldn't have been so bad if you'd told a friend, or something…' I thought about the letter on its way to Denille, but decided to keep this to myself… 'but to talk about it to… *him*! He robbed me once. Now he'll rob me again. You broke your promise, Candice. How could you do that? How can you live with yourself?'

'I am *not* going to rob you, Jim. Would I be here if that was the case?' said Rich Uncle Brian. 'And don't raise your voice to Candice.'

'I am her father,' yelled Dad. 'Don't tell me what I can or cannot do.'

The waiter approached once more, but did an about-turn and headed off to another table. The chances of getting my dim sims were shrinking by the moment.

'Let's talk business, then,' said Rich Uncle Brian. 'I know you don't like me, Jim. That's fine. You don't have to like a business partner.'

'Like I'd go into business with you, Brian!' replied Dad. At least he'd called him Brian. Was this progress?

'And another thing. How dare you give Candice money for a holiday? How *dare* you? Vicky and I felt…I can't describe it. Filthy.'

RUB leaned over and lowered his voice.

'I don't want to talk about that, Jim. Not here. Not now. Not in front of…' He nodded his head towards me.

'Candice,' I said, but no one paid any attention.

'Good. Don't talk about it. That's great, because I don't want to hear. Leave, Brian.'

Rich Uncle Brian stroked his moustache. He glanced at me. For a moment I thought he might jingle some coins, but he didn't.

'You stubborn mule, Jim,' he said. 'Okay. Listen. The trip to New Orleans was never going to be funded by Candice's trust fund. As if I would do that.'

'So who was going to pay?'

'I was.'

'I take it back,' said Dad. 'I don't feel filthy. I feel violated. I will die before I accept charity from you, Brian.'

'Not charity,' said RUB. 'Business, Jim. Just business. There is a social network convention in New Orleans in October. All the big players will be there. I want you to go. As a representative of my company.'

'You're crazy.'

'Here's what I'm offering,' replied Rich Uncle Brian. 'Unlimited use of my company resources to develop your program. As much time as you need. A team of programmers. Come on, Jim. How long is it going to take you to write this by yourself? Someone else will get in first, even if you register a patent. You know how quickly the world of computing changes. It will eat you up and spit you out. You need me, Jim. And you know it.'

Dad's eyes narrowed and I got the impression Rich Uncle Brian's words had struck a nerve. I sat back. Wherever this conversation was going, I would be a witness only. I just wish I had a dim sim to nibble on.

'And, what?' said Dad. 'I hand over all rights to you? Forget it. I'll go to one of your rivals.'

'You retain full copyright. You get ninety percent of profits, I get ten. You become a director of the firm. On a salary. The lawyers can thrash out the details later. That's the bare bones of the offer and you're welcome to check whether my rivals can match it. But they can't. Come on, Jim. Think about it, man. This is business.'

Dad thought. He also spoke. So did Rich Uncle Brian.

I didn't speak. I didn't do much thinking either. I wanted dim sims.

Dad and Rich Uncle Brian didn't become friends

over the next half hour, but when it was all over they shook hands.

We went to the car park and Rich Uncle Brian tousled my hair before driving off in his four-wheel drive. We climbed into Dad's white ute.

'Don't think I've forgiven you, Candice,' said Dad. 'Not yet.'

'I haven't forgiven you either, Dad,' I replied. 'You promised me lunch.'

I hummed for a couple of kilometres.

'So does this mean we are going to New Orleans after all?' I said.

Dad pulled at an earlobe.

'Maybe,' he said. 'Probably,' he added.

I smiled. Some things are better even than dim sims. Not many, mind you.

~

Late that night I heard Mum's bedroom door open. I listened as she moved into the kitchen and then there was a scrape as the back door opened. There's no mistaking the sound. The wood has warped and doesn't fit the frame. I hopped out of bed and padded along the corridor. The back door was ajar. I put on my slip-on shoes and went into the garden. Mum was sitting on a concrete wall bordering a flower bed. Her head was turned to the night sky.

I sat beside her. She glanced at me and smiled, then returned her gaze to the blackness above. I looked as well. The night was nailed on with hard, bright stars.

'Where is she, Candice?' asked Mum.

Dad had shown me where to look. I pointed.

'She's there, Mum,' I said. 'Sky is there.'

Z

IS FOR ZERO-HOUR

....

Dad had offered to take me to Douglas's house on Sunday, but circumstances prevented it. For one thing, he'd bought himself a new remote-controlled plane and wanted to test it. For another, he had arranged a meeting with Rich Uncle Brian. They were going sailing to finalise the details of their business plan. Over buckets of vomit, probably. So I took my bicycle with three wheels. It was a beautiful day with scarcely a cloud in the sky. I didn't fall off once.

I fell off twice.

I hadn't used the bike since I'd stopped visiting the ravine following Douglas's promise he wouldn't kill himself. You need to practise things like that. Bike riding, I mean. Not killing yourself.

The facsimile parents were pleased to see me. I wondered if they were also thrilled about me becoming their daughter-in-law, though I wasn't sure Douglas had told them yet. Maybe that was going to be raised over lunch.

Which was great, incidentally. It was things you could pick at – biscuits, cheese, dips, crusty bread and fresh fruit. Strawberries. I love the way they explode sweetly in your mouth when you crunch down. After lunch, facsimile father Joe put an arm around Douglas Benson From Another Dimension's shoulder.

'Let's leave the women to clear up, son,' he said. 'I need help cutting firewood.' I worried about women cleaning while men played with axes [I am a modern girl], but wasn't in a position to object. Douglas seemed even less impressed. I suspected he would have preferred pondering problems of quantum physics or experimenting with harp melodies to wielding axes. He scowled. He scratched the knobbly bits on his head. But he went.

This left me alone with facsimile mother, Penelope. I felt stressed. It's not often you wash dishes in total silence [unless it's with a family member. So actually, it *is* often]. True, I'd met her before, but even so. And it's impossible to write notes when your hands are covered in washing-up suds. I've tried. The ink runs.

'I want to thank you, Candice, for what you've done for Douglas,' said facsimile Penelope when the final plate was dried. I didn't know what to say so I just nodded. We sat at the kitchen table. She placed her chin into a cupped hand and examined its wood grain. The table, not the hand.

'Things have not been easy since his accident,' she continued.

Possibly I raised an eyebrow [it's not out of the question I raised two] because she continued. 'He hit his head about a year ago. Jumping out of a tree, of all things. At first we thought it was concussion. That's what the doctors said. But concussion passes. This didn't. He wasn't the same boy at all. Quite a personality change, really.' She scratched a fingernail over a wet patch on the table. 'Before, he was…well, a typical thirteen-year-old. Since the accident, he's been more… gentle.' She laughed. 'It must have knocked some sense into him as well, because his school grades have improved enormously.'

'Fancy,' I said. I had to say *something*.

'Yes,' said facsimile Penelope. 'The doctors told us a blow to the head can sometimes produce personality changes. Sometimes it's permanent. Sometimes the old character resurfaces after a time. Anyway, now he seems to have these *delusions...*'

I didn't know what to say. Humming was antisocial under the circumstances, so I kept quiet.

'Anyway, he had friends before the accident, but since...there's been no one. Until you. And that's why I want to thank you, Candice. For being a friend to my son.'

I was relieved. I hadn't looked forward to discussing tiered cakes, trousseaus and reception venues.

'You're welcome,' I said.

And she was.

~

Douglas and I had a great afternoon. We walked to the ravine. I even plucked up the courage to dangle my ankles over the edge, though I kept one arm wrapped around a tree so tightly it cut off my circulation.

'This is it, Candice,' said Douglas, gazing over the river far below. 'The day I return. I know it. I can feel it.'

'The maths work, then?' I asked.

'Absolutely,' he said. 'I can't tell you how good it will be to get back.'

'You can,' I said.

'No. I mean, it's difficult to find the words. My world is great, Candice. It looks much like this, but in many ways it is very different. Mum and Dad will have missed me. I can't wait to explain to Mum what I've discovered about gravity and string theory. She is going to be so excited. And afterwards, I can listen to Dad play his Aeolian harp as we watch the suns go down.'

I was going to ask about Aeolian harps, but his last words gave me pause.

'Suns?' I said.

'Yes. Two of them. They set within half an hour of each other. It's the biggest difference between this world and mine.'

I couldn't think what to say, but something was expected.

'Who'd have thought?' I said.

'Well, me for one,' replied Douglas. 'The thing is, Candice, I'm going to miss you so much. I can't tell you.'

'You can,' I said.

'No. I mean it's difficult to find the words. I love you, Candice. It breaks my heart to think I'll be leaving you. But I can't think of a way to take you along. When I get back I'll talk it over with Mum. She might have some ideas. And if it's at all possible, I'll be back. Promise you'll wait for me.'

I couldn't think of anything to say, but something was expected.

'Righty ho,' I said.

After that, we said little. Douglas Benson From Another Dimension stared into the distance and I hummed, but it was just time-filling. Eventually, we wandered back to the house. It was six-fifteen.

I gathered around the tree-portal/passport. It *is* possible for one person to gather because I did it. Douglas shinned up the tree-passport's trunk and settled on a branch about five metres from the ground. He shifted his feet to maintain balance and glanced at his watch. I glanced at mine. He glanced at his. I glanced at mine. We were good at this. One minute to go. I thought maybe I should make a speech, but couldn't think of anything to say. *Bon voyage* seemed rather weak.

'Forty-five seconds, Douglas,' I said in place of a speech.

'Forty-two,' he replied.

We counted down together. When we got to five, he put his hands above his head, like an Olympic high-diver. At zero, he jumped.

He hit his head on the way down. I heard the thunk of head on branch. He landed off balance, tottered, and fell to the ground. I rushed over. He lay on his side and his eyelids fluttered. A broad gash ran from his right eyebrow to his right ear. It oozed blood. I cradled his head in my arm before I realised that I shouldn't have.

I'd done a first-aid course last year. I should have left him and gone for help. But I wasn't thinking clearly.

'Douglas?' I said. 'Are you okay?'

He moved his tongue over his lips and his eyelids fluttered some more.

'Douglas?'

He opened his eyes. They didn't quite focus. It was like he was looking through me.

'What the…?' he muttered.

'You're okay,' I said, though I had no idea if that was true. In fact, I opened my mouth to correct myself, but didn't get the chance. His eyes roamed my face.

'Who are you?' he croaked.

What happened next was a blur. Douglas's eyes rolled back in his head. Facsimile Penelope came rushing out. There was crying and yelling. There was bustle. There was a phone call. An ambulance arrived ten minutes later in a blaze of flashing lights. Douglas was stretchered into it. His facsimile parents scrambled into the back. The ambulance left in the same blaze of flashing lights. I watched it disappear down the track. After a minute I couldn't even hear the siren. The silence was…oppressive.

~

I rode home very slowly and didn't fall off once. Or twice. There had been too much falling today. The trip gave me the opportunity to go over in my head what I had witnessed. I ran the scene over and over and I still wasn't sure. You see, for a moment there, as Douglas was plummeting to earth, I thought I saw him flicker. Or shimmer. It was the tiniest fraction of a second. Maybe I blinked.

Or maybe I'd seen Douglas Benson From Another Dimension going home.

Mum rang Douglas's facsimile mother later that day [I'm no good on the phone to people I don't know well]. The news was good. Douglas had recovered consciousness and seemed fine. He'd had x-rays and other tests and they'd come out normal. The hospital was keeping him in for a few days for observation, but the general opinion was that he'd just have a bad headache for a day or two. Mum sent our best wishes.

The next few days were strange. School felt lonely and home was very different. Dad spent lots of time with Rich Uncle Brian and he'd come home from these meetings in a very good mood. Once or twice we went to the park and flew his plane. He made jokes *all* the time. Mum wasn't in her bedroom nearly as much. Once I caught her looking at a book about New Orleans. She had a dreamy smile on her face.

Dreamy smiles were becoming common in the Phee household.

Thursday lunchtime. I sat in my specially reserved library chair, ate a sandwich and flicked through a new dictionary that had just arrived. I was impressed with it. It had new words and that is a good thing.

Douglas tapped me on the knee. He had a bandage round his head and I was impressed with that too. It framed his knobbly bits beautifully.

'Hi Candice,' he said.

I struggled with my response. Should I say 'Hello Douglas Benson From Another Dimension' or 'Hello Douglas Benson'? Who was I talking to? I examined his interesting face. His eyes still crowded towards the middle. His nose was still larger than you'd wish if designing it from scratch. His eyebrows remained hairy caterpillars. His knobbly bits appeared unchanged. And then a small light bulb appeared over my head. Actually, it didn't. I speak metaphorically.

If Douglas Benson From Another Dimension had gone home then *this* Douglas Benson wouldn't know who I was. My logic was sound. I put it down to reading the dictionary and the complete works of Charles Dickens. This undoubtedly hones brain power.

'Hello, Douglas Benson From Another Dimension,' I said. 'It didn't work, then.'

'What?'

'Your portal/passport.'

He knelt before me and his eyes flashed with excitement.

'Wrong, Candice,' he said. 'It did work. It worked beautifully.'

'Oh,' I said. Maybe my brain wasn't very honed.

'I've come back,' he continued. 'I spent a couple of days with Mum and Dad and then I returned to this world.'

'Fancy,' I said.

'I came back for you,' he said. 'I want you to travel with me across dimensions.'

'Hmmm,' I said. I thought this was an appropriate remark under the circumstances.

'Will you, Candice? Will you? Mum and Dad are so looking forward to meeting you.'

'I thought you couldn't think of a way.'

'I couldn't. But Mum did. We worked it out together.'

'Does it involve trees?'

'Yes.'

'Then I can't, Douglas,' I replied.

His face fell. 'Why?'

'Because I am afraid of heights. I cannot climb the tree-passport. Even if I could, I wouldn't be able to jump from it.'

He got to his feet and paced. His hands clenched

into fists. He even tried to pull at his hair, but it was so short he couldn't get a grip. Finally, he returned.

'I'll think of another way, Candice,' he said. 'A way that doesn't involve trees.'

'Or heights of any kind?'

'Or heights of any kind. It will be difficult. It will be very difficult. But I'll do it. I swear to you, Candice. I *will* do it. You'll just have to give me time.'

'Righty ho,' I said. 'Consider time to be given.'

He left after that. Douglas told me he had only come to school to see me and that the doctors had instructed him to take the week off. I watched him walk down the library stairs. To be honest, I wasn't too sorry to see him leave. The new dictionary was calling to me and I wanted to look up the word *delusion* again.

Walking home from school, I heard the sound of a motorbike. I stopped because it sounded like the motorbike was on the pavement. It was. So was I.

It stopped next to me and the rider lifted up the visor on her helmet. It was a postie and not just any postie. Facsimile Penelope.

'Hello, Candice,' she said. 'I thought it was you.'

'Hello,' I said.

'I'm so sorry we didn't get a chance to say goodbye on Sunday,' she continued. 'But what with the ambulance and everything…'

'That's okay.' I said. 'I'm glad Douglas is better.'

'Thank you, Candice. I can't tell you how relieved we are.'

'You can,' I said.

Facsimile Penelope looked puzzled, but then delved into her satchel. 'I nearly forgot. I have a letter for you.'

'For me?'

She handed it over. It had a blue sticker with 'Air Mail' printed on it. And an American stamp. Facsimile Penelope drove off in a thin cloud of blue smoke. I ripped open the envelope and unfolded the single sheet.

~

Dear Candice,

Hey, I am so sorry I haven't replied to your letters! The thing is, the address was wrong. All your letters were delivered to my neighbor, Mr Singlebaum, who has the apartment above ours. And he's been in Europe for the last year. He got back yesterday and brought them to our apartment.

I just about died laughing reading your letters. You are either one cool chick or you're completely and utterly mad. Who knows? Maybe you're both. Or maybe you're deliberately weird. A lot of my friends reckon I'm crazy, so I guess we'll get along. I have

so much catching up to do, but I thought
I'd just get this note off to you. Expect
heaps of letters over the coming months.

Thanks for the geography lesson, incidentally.
Who'da thought Canada was to the north of
us (I'm kidding, by the way)? And, yeah, I've
got a boyfriend who's our school's quarterback.
This Douglas dude sounds unbelievably weird.

Gotta go and catch the post.
Your penpal,
Denille

~

I looked up at the cloudless sky. I am fairly sure there was a dreamy smile on my face. As I said, you can't move for dreamy smiles in the Phee household these days.

I love it when things work out. And it suddenly occurred to me that I had finished the Alphabet Autobiography as well. Hurrah! Miss Bamford would be pleased [and possibly astonished at its length]. But finishing it also made me just a little sad. I'm not a fan of things ending. That's probably why I just go round and round.

I'm already thinking of my next chapter. 'A Is For Aardvark.'

What do you think?

BARRY JONSBERG's young adult novels, *The Whole Business with Kiffo and the Pitbull* and *It's Not All About YOU, Calma!* were short-listed for the Children's Book Council Awards, Book of the Year, Older Readers. *It's Not All About YOU, Calma!* also won the Adelaide Festival Award for Children's Literature, *Dreamrider* was short-listed in the New South Wales Premier's Awards for the Ethel Turner prize, and *Cassie* (Girlfriend Fiction) was short-listed for the Children's Peace Literature Award. *Being Here* won the Queensland Premier's Young Adult Book Award 2011 and was short-listed for the 2012 Prime Minister's award.

Barry lives in Darwin with his wife, children and two dogs. His books have been published in the USA, the UK, France, Poland, Germany, China, Hungary and Brazil.